REFLECTION

BOOKSHOP

REFLECTIONS FROM A BOOKSHOP WINDOW

CLIVE LINKLATER

Illustrated by David Hobbs

BREESE
BOOKS
LONDON

First published in 1996 by
Breese Books Ltd
164 Kensington Park Road, London W11 2ER, England

ISBN: 0 947533 01X

Printed and bound in Great Britain by
Itchen Printers Ltd, Southampton

Monday 8th October

> *FOR SALE.*
> *Small freehold farm, comprising a*
> *farmhouse, outbuildings, and about*
> *4½ acres of excellent land.*
> *Price £1,200.*

I know there's a property slump but this is ridiculous. I turn the page.

> *FOR SALE.*
> *Good modern semi-detached house,*
> *with small flower garden. Contains*
> *two sitting rooms, six bed and*
> *dressing rooms, house-keepers room,*
> *kitchen and offices.*
> *Price £950.*

I fold the book shut. Its paper cover is darkened and brittle as if from proximity to a fire. Across the top is an engraving of a steam train and beneath it reads -

The Tunbridge Wells Railway
Time Table Compendium
incorporating
The Monthly
House & Estate
Circular
of
Messrs Brackett & Son
Auctioneers & Estate Agents
27 High Street, Tunbridge Wells

At the bottom of the page, the date - December 1889. I reach over to my newspaper just to make sure - October 8th 1990.

Things may be slow in the property market but surely they'll have gone by now.

The lady who brought it into the shop had found it in an aunt's loft. I bought it, somewhat reluctantly (because of the bad condition), for £2.50. She said she needed the money for that evening's meal.

I thought briefly of phoning Messrs Brackett and Son to see if they wished to buy the book. (Yellow Pages confirmed they were still in business. I'm not surprised, selling property at prices like that.) The more I mentally rehearsed the conversation with an estate agent's receptionist, the more daunting the prospect became.

"I'm phoning up to see if you would like to purchase a list of properties which you had for sale in December 1889."

"I'm sorry Sir, would you mind repeating that."

"Yes. I'm phoning up to see if you would like to purchase a list of properties which you had for sale in December 1889."

"If you'd like to hold, Sir, I'll put you through to our other department."

I'm sure if they had agreed to a purchase, the whole process would have taken six months and involved me in about £350 of legal expenses.

I phone James. James is to bookselling what Fred Housego is to taxi driving; a cut above the rest and he knows it.

"It's very interesting, James; lists all the properties for sale and to let in Tunbridge Wells; loads of adverts. I'm sure if you phoned Messrs Brackett and Son, you'd sell it straight away." (He probably will. He makes money because he actually does the things I only think about doing.)

I continue my sales patter for what seems like half an hour. Sweat begins to form on my forehead. I explain how it's a very important document in the history of an estate agency. I am a born salesman.

"I'll take it," interrupts James. "I can probably turn it over to someone who collects railway timetables. I'll give you five pounds."

And so the journey has begun. For years I have pondered the idea and done nothing. Now the first link in the chain is complete.

Normally when I sell a book for five pounds, I keep £2.50 to reinvest in another book, and watch as my wife runs off with the other £2.50.

I thus end each financial year in much the same position as I started it: with £2.50 in my pocket.

This year, though, it might just be different. This year I have a plan.

The theory is simple -

Take an initial outlay of £2.50.

Buy a book and sell it for £5.

Buy a book with the £5 and sell it for £10.

Buy a book with the £10 and sell it for £20.

Each time the book is sold, take the proceeds and reinvest it in another book.

The idea is to continue the process for a year and see how far the value of the book increases.

In theory, double the value of the book each month and you have a book worth, let me see - 5,10,20,40,80.........£10,240.

And it works. I have proved it. I slip the £5 into my pocket. Tomorrow I shall spend it.

At the back of my mind, I am already wondering where you buy a book worth £10,240.

Tuesday 9th October

The next move is vital. A mistake now could jeopardise the whole exercise. I must spend the money wisely. I must not rush out and squander it on the first book I find that happens to cost five pounds. I finger the five pound note in my pocket (that's my excuse anyway).

"Restraint, restraint," I murmur to myself as I approach the door to 'Sam's Secondhand Book Emporium'.

"Any books for five pounds, Sam?" The words almost tumble over each other in their headlong rush.

"Only 'Antique Cats for Collectors'."

"I'll take it."

The book is in my possession, and the five pound note snuggling contentedly in Sam's till, before I realise what I have done. At the back of my brain, I notice a persistent mantra continuing to echo - 'Restraint, restraint.'

I glance at the book. On its cover an ornamental cat looks me straight in the eye. Its face is dominated by an oversized smug grin. It seems to be saying - "who's been a silly boy then?"

I glance at Sam. The identical grin beams back.

I read the title more slowly.

'Antique.....Cats.....for.....Collectors'

What are antique cats? At what age does a cat become antique? Who collects antique cats? Do the people who collect antique cats want books on the subject? Why have I bought a book on antique cat collecting? Can I have my five pounds back please Sam?

Perhaps, even as I write, an elderly gentleman is phoning round the secondhand bookshops in Yellow Pages, searching for a book called 'Antique Cats for Collectors'. I check for the author's name; could it just possibly be J.R. Hartley?

If he phoned and offered me £2.50, I'd probably take it and start again.

It is, of course, possible to sell anything. I once bet another bookseller I could take the dullest book in the shop and, by imaginative sales technique, persuade someone to buy it.

'British Friesian Herd Book Vol 39' had been in stock since I opened eight years previously. Regulars would see it, comment, "I see you've still got the British Friesian Herd Book Vol 39," and collapse amid torrents of uncontrollable laughter.

Even to move it was to run the risk that the whole structure of the shop depended, somehow, on that particular book remaining in that particular position. I pulled at it nervously. As I did so, a sleepy eyed insect emerged and peered over the top of the spine. It clambered shakily onto the shelf, and proceeded towards the fiction section, followed by a well regimented procession of smaller insects. They hesitated briefly by a copy of Priestly's 'Angel Pavement', before squeezing beneath the cover of a Readers Digest condensed novel, there, no doubt, to remain undisturbed for the next eight years.

I had an emotional attachment to the 'British Friesian Herd Book Vol 39'. It was with some reluctance that I positioned the book in the window next to a sign which read -

STRICTLY NOT FOR SALE UNDER ANY CIRCUMSTANCES

I had not quite reached my desk, when an elderly gentleman entered and approached waving a sheet of paper.

"That is Vol 39 of the British Friesian Herd Book in the window isn't it?" he enquired.

"That's right."

"I'd like to buy it."

"It's not for sale under any circumstances."

His face reddened. He opened the sheet of paper and pushed it towards me.

"It's the only one I need to complete my set."

To save him from what seemed like an imminent heart attack, I eventually agreed to sell it to him for five pounds. The bet brought me another five.

Surely the man who sold the 'British Friesian Herd Book Vol 39' can sell anything. I pick up my copy of 'Antique Cats for Collectors'.

The expression on the cat's face remains unchanged.

Wednesday 10th October

I find my copy of the 'Bookdealer' (a weekly trade paper listing books wanted by the secondhand booktrade): I open it on the first page. Is it just possible, could it just be, that 'Antique Cats for Collectors' will be in someone's list? I place my finger at the top of the page and begin to read -

More Queer things about Japan.

The Complete Goggler.

Endemic Flora of Tasmania (any odd volumes).

Management and Treatment of Elephants.

The Complete Leg Spin Bowler.

Chilean Medico - Social Reality.

Mr & Mrs Quiz Book.

Transvestite Vampire.

Atlas of Female Anatomy (text only).

The History of Wesleyan Methodism in Grantham.

The Edible Ornamental Garden.

Unicorns I have known.

The Fat Man in History.

Lady Macleans Book of Sauces and Surprises.

Anglo Saxon cemeteries.

Winnie the Pooh is a capitalist lackey.

Do Androids dream of electric sheep.

Building the 1½" Scale Alchin Traction Engine.

What a strange and varied creature the human being is.

(That's not a book title, merely a reflection on the books people read.) In comparison, people who collect antique cats seem positively normal.

No one is advertising for 'Antique Cats for Collectors'. Perhaps the fashion in antique cat collecting has now passed its peak. I feel cheated to think my money would have been better invested in a Mr & Mrs Quiz Book.

On page 25 I discover a glimmer of hope -

M.C. ASTON - Earlsdon, Coventry.
Cats, Cats, Cats, Cats. Please quote all books relating to cats.-Anything catty whatsoever.
Cats, Cats, Cats.

I think it is safe to assume that M.C. Aston of Earlsdon, Coventry, is a bookdealer who knows exactly the category of animal in which they are interested. It is clearly not dogs.

M.C. Aston, if you are a woman, I am in love already.

I ignore the phone number. If the love affair is to end in heartbreak, I shall at least postpone the day of reckoning. I write -

Dear M.C. Aston,
With reference to your Bookdealer ad 4/10/90, I can offer the following - "Antique Cats for Collectors" by K. McClinton. Price £11 Post Free.

I give no indication of my newfound affection. As I release the letter into the post box, it is with a feeling more of resignation than of hope.

I return to my everyday life and wait.

Thursday 11th October

Everyday life means there is still a living to be made. Everyday life means there are shelves to be filled, mouths to be fed. Everyday life means there is a book sale to be attended on Saturday, but don't, whatever you do, tell a soul.

Memories of the last book sale are still vivid. I caught the early train to make sure I was the first to arrive. Through the church hall window, I could see the trestle tables straining under their load.

'TEAS 15p, ALL BOOKS 20p,' read the sign.

I placed myself on the stone step, where I decided the head of the queue should be.

When I saw the vicar approaching, I lowered my head, as though by doing so I made myself invisible.

"Are you a dealer?" he enquired.

I looked up with a "who me?" expression on my face. Years of experience meant the reply came with well rehearsed precision.

"No, no, I just like to read a lot."

People, I have learnt, refer to dealers in the same tone as they refer to large dollops of particularly unsightly dog excrement sticking to the sole of their shoe.

I have arrived at book sales, only to find a notice - NO DEALERS ADMITTED - pinned to the door.

How, you might ask, provided you did not walk in with a "Hi, I'm your local bookdealer," would they recognise you as such? They would, believe me, they would.

I have been to car boot sales in heavy disguise (I have shaved and cleaned my teeth), and still as I clamber amid boxes of Mills and Boons, I can hear the whispers, "He's a dealer, he's a dealer," as though saying, "He's got rabies, he's got rabies."

I didn't realise when I became a bookdealer that, in terms of public esteem, they ranked somewhere between plumbers and Jehovahs Witnesses. You could be the worst doctor in the world, fail to cure a single patient in your life, and still the words "He's a doctor" would be spoken with reverential awe. You could be the greatest bookseller in the world, and the best you could hope for in terms of social status would be parity with a roadsweeper.

There have been times when I have almost broken down and cried, "But I'm only trying to make a living."

The vicar was not convinced by my denial.

"That's a shame. I thought you might have liked to get in early and have a look around."

I had lied to a vicar, and that had been a foolish thing to do. I decided to repent immediately.

"Er, when I said I wasn't a dealer, er, what I should have said is, I am a bit of a dealer."

The vicar smiled a forgiving smile. Perhaps there is a God after all.

"Come in and have a look round then, before the crowds arrive."

He pushed open the door; I followed meekly like a disciple.

Inside, I learnt how a pig feels rolling in mud. Each table was laden with treasures. I began to make a pile on the floor of the books that I would want to buy. It occurred to me that here, in a Bexhill church hall, on an overcast Saturday morning, I was about to make my fortune. It was like first sex; long anticipated, yet hard to believe that it was actually happening.

Outside I saw a bedraggled line of dealers had gathered on the pavement. I moved closer to the window and gave them an obscene gesture of triumph. Their obscene gestures in reply moved down the queue like a badly timed Mexican wave. It started to rain.

My concentration returned to the books. As my pile of books increased, so did my dreams of wealth. The hand that gripped my shoulder startled me like an electric shock.

"You shouldn't be in here."

I turned to be confronted by the most enormous woman I had ever seen.

"But the vicar....."

"No arguing."

Her voice was as deep as her body was large. Her hand propelled me mercilessly towards the door. She was the irresistable force, and I was the highly moveable object.

Outside the rain was still falling. The crowd of dealers greeted my appearance with a chorus of unconcealed delight. The triumph now was theirs.

On the train journey home, I checked my booty: four Dornford Yates novels, an Agatha Christie omnibus, and a life story of Muhamed Ali. Inside the hall, my reserved pile had melted away like an iceberg in a heatwave. It would be a long time before I could forget the feel of that hand on my shoulder. It would be a long time before I could forgive that enormous woman.

Saturday 13th October

Booksales, from that day on, have been high on my list of priorities. Just momentarily I had believed myself to be a rich man, and it has given me hope. This latest book sale has been in my thoughts since I saw it advertised in a Crowborough shop window a week ago.

BOOK SALE
CROWBOROUGH CHURCH HALL
BARGAINS GALORE

I have seen no mention of it in the press. My hope is the other dealers will not have heard about it. I have mentioned it to no one.

I take the train to Lewes and the bus to Crowborough. After a thirty minute walk, I find the hall at the side of an open common. The journey in all has taken three hours.

Ideally, I would like to ascertain the layout inside the hall. I could then plan my movements like a military campaign; first stop would be antiquarian books, then natural history, then travel..... I attempt to peer through the windows but the curtains are pulled shut. So far, though, so good; no sign of any other dealers. I peer anxiously up and down the road.

About twenty minutes before opening, a car pulls up; to my relief, a small girl in a Brownie uniform gets out and moves to stand next to me in an embryonic queue. A light drizzle has become somewhat heavier. My Brownie companion produces an umbrella and, from its shelter, stares up sympathetically as raindrops move steadily down my face and into my beard.

She is joined, soon after, by an almost identical Brownie, and they talk excitedly in special Brownie language. At intervals they look towards me and smile. The queue soon grows to six, five of whom are Brownies. Apart from the fact that I am three times their size, bearded, male, out of uniform, and most obviously a dealer of some description, I do not feel particularly conspicuous. Mechanically almost, I continue to search approaching roads for other dealers. The only figures moving in our direction are more Brownies.

With five minutes to go till opening, the queue stretches all the way to the main road. I am unmistakably the only non Brownie in the queue. A lady Brownie comes out and pins a notice to the door -

CROWBOROUGH BROWNIES
5TH ANNUAL BOOKSALE

"Open in five minutes girls," she announces.

"And gentlemen," she adds, staring me straight in the eye.

A small squeal of delight shivers through the queue. As a gesture, I attempt my own small squeal. I discover it is not a noise that fits easily within my vocal range.

I could, of course, at this point, turn towards the bus station and walk away. No one knows who I am. No one knows where I come from. Next year they would be able to talk in Brownie language, about the strange bearded man, who queued for hours at last years book sale and left just as the doors were about to open.

Instead, an unseen force holds me in the queue and, once the door opens, deposits me in front of a single rickety trestle table displaying an assortment of Bunty annuals and Enid Blyton novels. It is a situation that tests my self composure to its limits.

I have anticipated this moment for a week; I have travelled for three hours; I have queued for an hour in the pouring rain, and I now have to spend the next ten minutes feigning appreciation of this display of Mr Men Stories and Ladybird read it yourself books.

I eventually pay for a copy of 'Thomas the Tank Engine and Friends', tell the lady it is just what I was looking for, and start out on the return journey through rain which is now falling more heavily than ever.

As I walk down the pathway, I genuinely cannot decide whether to laugh or cry.

Monday 15th October

M.C. Aston is a woman. Driffield has told me. Her name is Maxine. If I had still been in love, it is a name that could only have added to the attraction. I decide not to tell Driffield about the Brownie book sale. I decide to talk about something not remotely connected with Brownies: it's bad enough having to dream about them all night long.

"I'm trying to sell a book called 'Antique Cats for Collectors'."

"There's a woman for cat books in......"

"Coventry?" I interject.

"That's it, she's called......."

"M.C. Aston."

"That's it, Maxine Aston. She's just sent me her catalogue."

At that first mention of the name, Maxine, a small shudder of anticipation passes through my vital organs. It is not a shudder of any longevity. Driffield is speaking in his best telephone voice.

"She's got a copy of 'Antique Cats for Collectors'. Apparently it's the definitive book on the subject. She wants £15 for it....... Hello, are you still there?"

My thoughts are whirring like a pocket calculator. She already has a copy of the book. She is only asking £15 for her copy. The chances of her paying £11 for mine are remote to say the least. A harsh truth is beginning to dawn.

I decide to change the subject to something less depressing.

"I went to a book sale in Crowborough on Saturday; it took me three hours to get there."

The flow of my narrative is hampered, somewhat, by unhealthy demands, on the part of Driffield, for detailed descriptions of small girls in Brownie uniforms. Even as I get to the more heartrending moments, where I am stranded alone in a strange town at the head of a queue of fifty Brownies, his only comment is - "That's great, that's great, tell me more about the Brownies."

I should, of course, know by now never to be surprised by Driffield.

I need, at this point, to take stock of my situation. The theory is simple; let me remind myself. I buy a book for £2.50 which I sell for £5. I buy a book for £5 which I sell for £10. And at the end of the year........

I have already visualised my advertisement in 'Exchange and Mart' -

'Interested in making money.
Want to change £2.50 into £10,000 within a year.
I did it, and so could you by sending off......'

The reality is proving more troublesome. I have bought a book for £2.50 and sold it for £5. I have bought a book for £5 which I would now be happy to sell for £5. The impact of my imaginary advert is becoming distinctly less dramatic -

'Not particularly interested in making money.
Want to take £2.50 and, after a year of extremely
hard work, change it into £5.
I did it, and so could you by sending off.......'

Tuesday 16th October

In the post this morning is a poll tax reminder, a Readers Digest Circular, and a postcard from Maxine. She would appear to be unique among bookdealers: she is willing to accept a modest profit. Her card is businesslike and concise -

"I accept your offer of 'Antique Cats for Collectors'
at £11 post free."

I dance round the kitchen floor until my pyjama bottoms fall down. (I do not think Maxine would be impressed.) My children cannot understand why selling a book for £11 gives me more pleasure than winning ½ million pounds in a Readers Digest prize draw (oh, the innocence of youth).

I feel lightheaded and reckless. I consider for a moment paying an instalment off my poll tax bill. The very thought is enough to bring me plummeting back to earth with a hefty bump.

Never before have I packed a book with such loving care as that which I bestow on 'Antique Cats for Collectors'.

As the grinning cat is submerged beneath brown paper, it is like saying goodbye to an old friend.

Friday 19th October

What qualities do I have that make me the ideal bookseller to carry out this experiment? Well firstly, of course, it was my idea. Not only did all the booksellers I know fail to think of the idea; they do not even seem particularly interested when I tell them about it.

The look they give me, as I explain my path to riches, is more one of sympathy than admiration. Only Driffield pesters me for more details: his curiosity fueled, it seems, by the mistaken belief that it has something to do with Brownies. (I made the mistake of introducing him to two unrelated concepts within a single phone call.)

I will need the quality of knowledge certainly. Knowledge with a capital K. I am renowned for my knowledge within the secondhand booktrade. (I don't have any.) Resourcefulness with a capital R. Adaptability with a capital A. Perseverance with a capital P. Knowledge, resourcefulness, adaptability, perseverance. K.R.A.P. There are people who would say that just about sums me up.

If any of these qualities applies to me, it is certainly perseverance. It is, after all, my family motto - `Persevere boy.' I often wish I had been born into a family with the motto - `Go out and have a bloody good time.' At least I wish someone had taken the trouble to translate `Persevere boy' into Latin.

Knowledge, resourcefulness, adaptability, and perseverance with a capital P. The time has come to spend my £10.

"Knowledge, resourcefulness, adaptability, perseverance", I mutter to myself as I approach the entrance to 'Sam's secondhand book emporium'.

The shop is empty. I assume Sam's wife has popped to the De La Warr pavilion to use the lavatory.

I decide on a final rendition of my newly devised mantra.

"K.R.A.P.," I exclaim as loudly as my lungs will permit me.

The face that emerges from behind the stack of science fiction paperbacks is that of Sam's wife.

"Oh Clive, it's you," she says, wiping the dust from her spectacles."Just for a moment you had me worried."

"Any books for £10, Jean?" I ask.

She looks at me as she might look at someone speaking in a particularly obscure foreign language.

"Books for £10?" she echoes.

I realise instantly the full implications of her retort. Sam does not sell books for £10. Trays of 20p bargains on the pavement; £5 'glossies' inside the locked glass cabinet; but nothing worth as much as £10. My journey is about to embark upon uncharted waters. As far as my experiment is concerned, 'Sam's secondhand book emporium' is history. I am about to go upmarket.

"Krap, krap, krap, krap," I chant as I head along Hastings seafront. The deeper into the old town I venture, the more subdued my chanting becomes. Compared to my normal haunts, it is a very posh area.

James' window display is in keeping with the poshness of its surroundings: no stray copies of the 'British Friesian Herd Book' here.

"Any of those books in the window £10, James?" I enquire.

He looks at me as he might look at someone who has just performed an extraordinarily loud fart.

It is clearly an enormous effort for him to produce a reply.

"No, not quite, Clive."

His patronising grin reminds me of Mrs Thatcher addressing a television interviewer. He is, though, clearly taken aback by the fact that I have £10 to spend.

I have moved upmarket so quickly that I am already out of my depth. (That sentence is awful, I rather like it.)

I am cheered by the news that James ended up having to give away the Messrs Brackett and Son circular that I sold to him for £5. To sell a book to a dealer, who then loses money on it, is the bookselling equivalent of the multiple orgasm.

I make my excuses and leave suitably humbled. I head towards Michael's. "Krap, krap, krap, krap," I chant as I head back in the direction from which I came. I remind myself of one of the three Billy Goats Gruff.

I like Michael. He's one of the small minority of booksellers who, like myself, actually has to make a living from bookselling. Most people who run secondhand bookshops have other means of support; rich wives, army pensions, money invested from profits made in the property boom. They don't actually give a toss whether you buy a book from them or not.

I am often asked if I would like to see something done about this unfair competition.

"Not at all," is my public utterance.

"Give them all a good kick in the goolies," is what I'd like to say.

Michael's goolies are in no danger whatsoever. By this stage in the week, his need to sell can border on the desperate. He watches customers handle books, in the same way a dog watches its master opening a can of dog food; with saliva dripping from the corners of his mouth.

There is a technique for buying books from Michael, and I like to think I am the master of it. I take from the shelves Vol.I of the 'Cambridge Modern History': inside is the price - '12 volumes only £30'. I look to make sure Michael is watching, before returning it to its original position. Michael's face drops like a bad case of diarrhoea. I pull out Vol II. I glance continually at Michael; Michael glances back at me. Neither of us says a word. We are involved in what is a well rehearsed process of silent haggling. The process continues until I have pulled out and replaced each volume in turn. There is a simple logic behind our unspoken communication: I would like the books, Michael would like my money. We are attempting to agree a mutually acceptable price without actually saying a word. This particular silent haggle has been unusually prolonged; I decide to call his bluff.

"Nothing for me today, Michael," I announce, and hurry out of the shop without a backward glance.

As I pass the outside of his window, I can hear a terrible wailing sound arising from the vicinity of Michael's desk. For anyone with even a scrap of human sensitivity, there is no alternative but to return immediately. I head for the nearest chip shop.

After a decent interval (and a disgusting bag of chips), I return to find Michael lying prostrate on the floor sobbing his heart out. I once more pull Vol I of the 'Cambridge Modern History' from the shelf.

"You interested in them?" gasps Michael, struggling for breath.

All told, I have been in the shop for over an hour; I have removed each volume in turn and examined it in minute detail; I have haggled silently and vigorously throughout, and Michael is still uncertain as to whether they are of interest to me or not. As proponents of silent haggling, one of us, at least, is losing our touch.

"Might be," I reply, adding to the tension.

"You can have them for £10."

If there is a winner and a loser in the process of silent haggling, I do believe its game, set and match to me. Judging by the exultant dance that Michael performs with the £10 held aloft above his head, I am not so sure he would agree.

•

Saturday 20th October

I have disposed of 'Antique Cats for Collectors' by intelligent use of the postal system, and I have reinvested the £10 in a set of history books that would give the average British postman a double hernia. "Resourcefulness, adaptability," I remind myself.

I lay the volumes across the top of my desk and begin to arrange them in numerical order - Vol. I, Vol II, Vol III, Vol IV...... All goes well until I find difficulty in locating Vol X. It is during the search for this errant volume, that I make the alarming discovery of a Vol. XIII. Even to a mathematical illiterate such as myself, the discovery of a volume thirteen in a twelve volume set is an obvious cause for concern.

I open Vol. I and examine Michael's inscription -

12 volumes only £30.

By placing an imaginary comma between the words 'Volumes' and 'only', the meaning is clear.

12 volumes, only £30.

It is a twelve volume set and the asking price is only £30. Exactly as I interpreted it in Michael's shop. Punctuation has never been my strong point, but I hesitantly push the imaginary comma along the sentence until it comes to a full stop (not literally) between the 'only' and the £30.

12 volumes only, £30.

The meaning is clear. There are only 12 volumes and there should be 13. I remember the war dance performed by Michael with the £10 brandished above his head. Its recall leaves me in no doubt, whatsoever, as to where the missing comma should have been positioned. I wonder if anyone has ever been prosecuted under the Trade Descriptions Act for poor punctuation.

I carried home in a cardboard box what I thought was a bargain to be exploited. The absence of a punctuation mark the size of your average sperm has transformed it into a problem to be solved.

"Resourcefulness, adaptability", I remind myself. If use of the G.P.O. is ruled out by the weight of the books, I shall have to resort to the long neglected 'window display method'.

My philosophy of window dressing is deeply entrenched. If you put good books in the window, people will keep coming in and asking to look at them. I did not become a bookseller in order to spend all day commuting between my armchair and the window display. I became a bookseller in order to sink into the comfort of my armchair in the morning, and stay there all day.

Anyway, if they're good books, they'll sell wherever you put them; so what's the point of wasting good window space displaying them. Far better, I always believe, to fill the window with the dullest books imaginable. Left in the shop they would never sell in a hundred years: put them in the window and any one sold is a bonus. I am famous in the booktrade for the awfulness of my window displays.

My customers are so in the habit of ignoring the contents of my window that, even if I persuaded Princess Diana to spreadeagle herself naked across the shop frontage, my regulars would walk straight past without realising she was there.

My window display at the moment consists of: an incomplete set of Walter Scott novels (half of them with their spines missing), 3 copies of the Guiness Book of Records (all for the year 1982), a signed copy of Edward Heath's book on sailing, an assortment of books on the royal wedding, and a biography of Margaret Thatcher (in Esperanto).

Amongst them I squeeze an incomplete set of the 'Cambridge Modern History'. Inside I have written -

12 volumes only, £20.

The comma is so small and faintly written, it almost requires a magnifying glass to find it.

Almost immediately, a young man hesitates on seeing them and enters the shop. He pulls the first volume from the window and approaches my desk. I notice droplets of saliva forming at the corners of my mouth.

"Is that the price? 12 volumes, only £20," he enquires.

"Er, 12 volumes only, £20," I inform him. "There's a comma between the 'only' and the '£20'."

He pulls a magnifying glass from his pocket and holds it above the book.

"So there is. I think I'll take them anyway."

As the door shuts behind him, I hold the £20 above my head and proceed round the shop in a triumphant war dance, not unlike Michael's.

Tuesday 23rd October

So far it has all been suspiciously easy; my only concern is that fate may have found out about my experiment and be attempting to take over. Common sense tells me I should be on my way to look for the next book; if fate is in charge, that book may already be looking for me.

I was once found by a Graham Greene signed first edition, in a Tunbridge Wells Oxfam shop. It is the only signed Graham Greene I have ever seen, and it found me on the only day I have ever gone out looking specifically for Graham Greene first editions.

I have accepted since that day that I am not totally in control of my own destiny.

I am wondering in what guise fate will next present itself, when a strangely dressed figure enters the shop and approaches my desk. It is Sam and he is carrying a box of books.

In a random universe, the books he is carrying could have any value. I buy them for twenty pounds.

I cannot remember if I am allowed to spend the money on more than one book. In future I shall make the rules up as I go along.

It occurs to me that, if I can catch this afternoon's post, I can advertise them for sale in next week's 'Bookdealer'. I write -

George Goldsmith Carter.
Forgotten Ports of England.1951. V.G. in dw   *£10. 00*
Fred. H. Crossley. Timber Building in England.
Batsford 1951. V.G. in dw   *£15.00*
R.V. Tooley. Maps and Map-Makers
Batsford 1949. V.G. in dw   *£15.00*
Barons Ballet Finale. Commentary by Arnold L Haskell
1958 V.G. in dw   *£9.00*
Post free. Offers considered.

(I once advertised a book for sale, price £8, offers considered, and an Irish bookdealer wrote back and offered £38. I have always assumed they must have gone out of business soon after. Who knows, another Irish bookseller might write and offer £200 for the four volumes.)

My medium sized son has come into the shop to ask for a penny for the guy. (It has become a family tradition that, in the autumn half term holiday, my children earn substantially more than I do.)

"Do us a favour Simon, pop home and fetch a first class stamp."

His reaction is instantaneous, and everything you would expect from a child brought up in a disciplined but caring environment.

"What's in it for me?"

We eventually agree on 20p, and he disappears up the road shouting "penny for the guy" as he goes. (I am sure the best way to make money would be to become a child again.)

It's while he's gone, that George walks in and offers £12 for 'Timber Building in England'. I accept with almost indecent alacrity and tear up my 'Bookdealer' list.

I explain to Simon why I no longer require the stamp. He explains to me why he is not going to give my 20p back.

I am left with three volumes and the feeling that fate is leaving it up to me to find a way of disposing of them. It now comes down to the basics; placing them on the shelves and waiting.

Any offers, of course, considered.

Wednesday 24th October

K.R.A.P.P.

Knowledge, resourcefulness, adaptability, perseverance and Patience with a capital P.

At ten the next morning, I lay the three books across the top of the unit that dominates the centre of the shop. I return to my armchair and fix my gaze on the books, which seem framed within a shaft of benevolent sunlight.

Distractions in secondhand bookselling can be manifold; I have had a customer set himself alight by standing too close to the gas fire; I have lost a customer beneath a ceiling that collapsed unexpectedly; I have had a drunk who decided that the handicraft section seemed as good a place as any to urinate. If all three were now to happen simultaneously, I do not believe my concentration would waver. (If all three were to happen simultaneously, it wouldn't do the lady buried under the ceiling any good, but the drunk could at least help extinguish the flames engulfing the customer stood next to him.)

At five past ten, a lady enters the shop, carrying something wet wrapped in newspaper. With an - "I'll just pop my fish on here a moment,"- she deposits her package on 'Hidden Ports of England' and heads for the etiquette section.

I forcibly reunite the lady and her fish, only to find a dog has wandered in behind her and is licking the aforementioned book with all the vigour of an animal that has not eaten for a month.

Meanwhile, a stream of other customers file past the three books, as though, by magic, they had been made invisible. What is wrong with people? How is it possible to go through life, and develop no interest whatsoever in either ballet, map-making, or the hidden ports of England (whatever they may be)?

Where normally I accept money with a grovelling servility, today I snatch it rudely and, motioning violently towards the centre of the shop, demand - "Are you quite sure there's nothing else I can interest you in?"

Patience, patience.

At twenty past ten, 'pain in the arse' enters. He moves unhesitatingly towards 'Barons Ballet Finale', and picks it up with as much finesse as a Dobermann Pinscher might pick up a rag doll. He yanks the book open at the first page, and pulls in two directions at once, as though engaged in a one man tug of war contest. The book disintegrates before my eyes like a greenhouse in a hurricane.

'Pain in the arse' moves towards the desk, kicking to one side shreds of dustwrapper that have fallen at his feet.

"Nothing much in stock at the moment, I see. Not that I've got any money on me anyway."

'Pain in the arse' has visited my shop about three times a day for the last six years. He has never bought a book. No, I lie; he once bought a book from the 10p rack outside, and ever since then his expression has seemed to indicate that I should be forever in his debt. (He actually brought the book back the next day and tried to sell it to my mother-in-law for 20p. I know because she showed it to me after she bought it.)

In his imagination, he believes that every time he enters my shop I am thinking -

"Oh great, what a stroke of luck, here comes 'pain in the arse'."

What I am actually thinking is -

"Oh hell, it's 'pain in the arse'."

He finally leaves the shop, knocking a two volume set of Shakespeare to the floor and slamming the door so hard the glass cracks.

As he passes the window, he sticks his thumb in the air and grins at me broadly. I refrain from responding with what I would consider an appropriate gesture and smile weakly back.

Patience, patience.

I piece together the remains of 'Barons Ballet Finale' as best I can and retire to my desk. I wait with all the composure I can muster. I sell two copies of the Guinness Book of Records and a biography of Margaret Thatcher from the window, but the three books that so preoccupy my thoughts remain unsold.

In my mind, I see daytime turning into night, autumn into winter. I check my watch; 10.45. Sod it, how much patience can a man be expected to have. I pick up the phone and dial James' number.

"I've got three books. I'll consider any offers."

James declines to offer anything for 'Barons Ballet Finale'. I think he is put off by the fact that the middle forty pages fall out when the book is gently shaken. He offers £18 for the others and leaves well satisfied, if a little concerned about a distinct fishy smell emanating from 'Hidden Ports of England'.

Despite having to deposit 'Barons Ballet Finale' in the wastepaper bin, my £20 investment has grown to £30. It will, though, be a wiser man who looks for a book to spend the money on. It will be a more cautious man who considers the best way to sell it.

Thursday 25th October

I wake in the morning full of determination.

Mrs Thatcher has, of course, given all small businessmen a new sense of direction. She has put a purpose in their stride. They know that in Thatcher's Britain, if they have the skill, the industry, and some good fortune, then the money they make as a result will be theirs. They also know that, if they make an awful lot of money, they might even have enough of it by the end of the year to pay their business rates and poll tax.

I search the morning paper optimistically for any reported assassination attempts on the Prime Minister's life. The nearest I come is the story of a man (not called Dennis) who attempts to poison his wife (not called Margaret) by putting rat poison in her cheese on toast.

I look dubiously at my boiled egg, before pointing out the story to my wife, who looks away in what I consider to be a highly suspicious manner. Her expression reminds me immediately of the case of the poisoned steam pudding.

My wife, I am sure, would be the first to concede that I did not marry her for her cooking. Ours is the only kitchen I know that has a government health warning fixed to the door. When we throw leftovers out to the birds, they throw them back. The case of the poisoned steam pudding is, though, as far as I know, the only serious attempt she has made on my life.

That I am alive today is due to the incredible sensitivity of the taste buds located at the tip of my tongue.

Even from a distance, it could not have been described as a steam pudding that bounced with health. It was, without doubt, a sickly looking steam pudding, and getting sicklier by the minute. I attacked the pudding with all the bravado of an old lady paddling in the English Channel (big toe first). I picked up the tiniest morsel on the edge of my spoon and transferred it to my mouth.

In my life I have heard many excruciating sounds, smelt many disgusting smells, seen many vile sights (you would expect all this living in our house), but never have my senses been so cruelly assaulted as they were by that morsel of steam pudding. It hit the far kitchen wall in what, had it taken place in official competition, would have been a world spitting record.

"Steam pudding not to your liking?" was my wife's considered observation.

The microscopic portion of steam pudding had been inside my mouth for a fraction of a millisecond, and yet, within an hour, it had set in motion (possibly not the best choice of words) the most violent bowel upheaval I had experienced since a sweltering afternoon in Calcutta.

Memories of that particular Calcutta afternoon come all too easily to mind. The trouble with being taken short in a foreign country is that you have no idea where the public toilets are. My travelling companion and I were sunbathing after a particularly spicy curry when, without warning, he leapt to his feet and ran in the direction of the horizon shouting -

"Oh my God, where's the nearest toilet?"

I laughed at his predicament and that was a mistake. An Indian curry does not move cautiously through the digestive system and ask to be let out. It proceeds with the speed of Ben Johnson on a high and attempts to expel itself with all the force of a space shuttle on take off. The countdown for this particular mission was unquestionably nearing its end = 10, 9, 8 . . . I picked up my belongings and headed quickly in the general direction of our hotel.

Within the first few strides I was able to calculate that, given the distance to the hotel, the increasing discomfort in my nether regions, and the speed at which I was moving, I was not going to make it. I accelerated into a trot; trotting made it worse. With each stride forward, my knees clasped tighter together, my body crouched lower to the ground. Crowds of locals gathered on the pavement, pointing at this strange English contortionist who waddled along the road like a deformed duck.

I cannot imagine what reservoirs of willpower I drew on to get me to the hotel steps. The groans I emitted as I crawled up the staircase would have made a werewolf's howling seem positively tuneful. I was going to make it though, . . . I was going to make it . . .

The queue for the toilet took up almost the entire length of the landing. As its members stood cross legged and doubled over towards the floor, there arose from their lips a terrible wailing cacophany of sound.

I gracelessly accepted the inevitable and, laying on the floor, let rip a long and very smelly scream.

It seems inconceivable that a crumb of steam pudding could now cause an equally distressing situation. But it did; and my anguish was compounded by the fact that it happened on the very day I started my new job as a roadsweeper.

My brush had barely encountered its first substantial lump of dogs doings, when the grumblings of discontent in my bowels began. I proceeded swiftly to the nearest public convenience, where I remained incommunicado for the next hour.

The remainder of my working day fell roughly into the same pattern; three minutes sweeping, followed by an hour of solitary confinement in the toilet cubicle. I only had to venture more than fifty yards from the lavatory, before I was called upon to rush wildly back in the direction from which I came.

At five o'clock, my supervisor turned up and commented that he had never seen the area round the public convenience looking so spotless.

"Why, you can almost see your reflection in the pavement," he added with uncalled for sarcasm. I headed home, unemployed again, to check on my wife's well being.

It was during one of my vigils in the lavatory, that my thoughts had turned towards the well being of my wife. Could I have been wrong in my initial assumption that the steam pudding was a deliberate attack on my life? Could I have misjudged her? Hadn't she polished off her own portion of steam pudding with some relish? Hadn't she reached out and grabbed my leftover pudding with the observation "I think I can find room for another portion." ?

I arrived home to find my children locked out of the house, and my wife sprawling on the kitchen floor in a state of near paralysis. It was more than a week before she was finally taken off the danger list.

So it was, after all, nothing more than a culinary disaster of quite unparalleled proportions. It did, though, give me a prejudiced view of my wife's cooking which survives to this day.

I look across from my paper and dubiously inspect this morning's boiled egg. I push it to one side.

"I really don't feel hungry this morning," I explain to my puzzled wife.

"Never mind, I'm sure I can manage another one," she splutters through a mouthful of egg yolk.

I head for the front door, with thirty pounds in my pocket, and little or no idea of where to spend it.

Friday 26th October

K.R.A.P.P.P.

No, this is not a continuing description of my exploits on a Calcutta hotel landing; it is simply my new look mantra with an extra P added on the end. If I carry on like this, by the time my experiment is finished, the mantra will be long enough to comprise a final chapter all by itself.

The extra P stands for people. It is not what you know, but who you know. It has suddenly occurred to me that I know nothing whatsoever about books worth more than £30. I do, however, have friends who know about £30 books. It is time to put their friendship to the test.

The first person I turn to for help is Sam. (A surprising choice, you may say, seeing as how, in the entire world, Sam is the only bookseller who knows less about expensive books than I do.)

The reason I turn to Sam is that he has just hit the jackpot. He has this week acquired the second best library to come onto the local market in the last ten years. (The best library came to me eight years ago, when I was given, for nothing, a quarter of a million books in a house in Sedlescombe.)

Booksellers search everywhere for books. They search in boot sales, jumble sales, auctions, charity shops (Sam searches the rubbish tip twice a day); and everywhere they search, they dream of hitting the jackpot. In every box of books that is brought into the shop, they hope they will find the books that will enable them to make their fortune.

The reality could not be more different. The books in the box are nearly always rubbish, and the problem of explaining this fact to their owner well known to all booksellers.

The explanation goes something like this -

CUSTOMER: "I've got this box of books for sale; they're Readers Digest condensed novels."

BOOKSELLER: "I'm awfully sorry, but I haven't got any use for that type of book at the moment."

CUSTOMER: "Why not?"

BOOKSELLER: "I've never been able to sell condensed novels, and anyway, they'd need to be in slightly better condition."

(To demonstrate, he picks up a volume and it falls to pieces in his hands.)

CUSTOMER: "What do you expect? They're more than four years old."

BOOKSELLER: "I'm awfully sorry, I really have no sale for them."

CUSTOMER: "What sort of books do you want then?"

BOOKSELLER: (Knowing from experience it is a question he has never known how to answer.) "Well.......er.......um.......let me see......."

CUSTOMER: "If you're not interested in books, you shouldn't have a notice in your window saying *BOOKS BOUGHT*."

It is a conversation that Sam must have endured many, many times; and each time he endured it, he must have done so in the hope that one day it would all be different.

Last week, a man walked into "Sam's Emporium" and offered him a library of mint conditioned books that eventually took Sam and ten helpers a couple of days to move. It was, by anybody's standards, a definite case of hitting the jackpot.

I know all this because Sam and I have a special relationship. Although Sam puts the cheaper books into the "Emporium", he brings the better books to me for my advice before selling them directly to the posher bookshops.

I decide it is time to take advantage of this special relationship.

"Sam, I wonder if you could look in your storeroom and find me a book for £30?"

I wait to see exactly how special the relationship is.

"I'll bring one in for you on Monday."

Good old Sam.

Monday 29th October

The book that Sam lays before me on Monday morning is 'Handbook of Engraved Gems' by C.W. King, second edition 1885. The impulsive side of my character tells me immediately that it is worth at least £30, and that I should buy it. The cautious side of my character tells me it is not worth any more than £30, and I should leave it well alone.

I know that Sam sold another copy to James last week for £20, and that James sold it from his window for £30. The fact that Sam is now attempting to sell the next copy for £30 is a perfect illustration of the lemming like nature of secondhand booksellers.

It is not, I think, widely realised, but it is a fact, that the brain circuitry of a secondhand bookdealer is based on the identical wiring system to that of a lemming.

A dealer in any other trade who sold an item for £20 would congratulate himself as the customer walked out of the shop.

"That's great, let's see how many others I can sell for the same price."

A secondhand bookdealer who sold a book for £20 would moan -

"Oh my God, what have I done? I've sold a book for £20 and I probably could have got £30."

The effect of this psychology is easy to predict. Next time a copy of the book turns up it will be priced at £30, and the price of every subsequent copy will increase until the book is so expensive it becomes unsaleable.

"I used to be able to sell this book, but no one seems to want it anymore," is a lament heard frequently in the secondhand book trade. Of course no one wants it, it's too bloody expensive.

The life cycle of the secondhand bookdealer is, in consequence, every bit as tragic as that of the lemming. Just as a lemming is programmed to fling itself headlong over the cliff edge, a bookdealer is programmed to end his days surrounded by overpriced books.

If, by chance, you discover a cheap secondhand bookshop, cherish it. Next year it will be overpriced and the year after next it will be a launderette.

I am disappointed to find that Sam is content to fling himself over the cliff edge with all the other lemmings. If I am to make a success of this experiment, I must resist the natural temptation to jump with him.

I return 'Handbook of Engraved Gems' to Sam. To judge from his puzzled expression, he clearly cannot understand why this particular copy should be more difficult to sell than the last.

Poor old Sam.

Friday 2nd November

In the next week, I visit every town within a 35 mile radius of Hastings. In places where on previous visits I left behind bookshops and antique shops, now I find estate agents and building society branches. (My only consolation is that all the estate agents look suicidal.) The sum total of my purchases is an incomplete set of Heron edition Dickens and a book on English coins that has been gnawed by a rat. I place them in the window, next to my only remaining copy of the Guiness Book of Records. I can find nothing worth anything remotely approaching £30.

On Friday I receive a phonecall that fills me with hope -

"I've got two copies of Mrs Beetons 'Book of Household Management', and a geography book signed by Florence Nightingale. Would it be alright to bring them in?"

Had anyone been in the shop as I answered the phone, they would have seen my eyes light up (not literally).

It transpires that the Mrs Beetons have been kept in someone's kitchen and used to chop up vegetables on. I am only able to offer £15 for the two. The Florence Nightingale item is altogether more promising.

I decide to impress the owner of the books with some erudite conversation.

"She died while still in her twenties, you know."

Instead of looking aghast at the depth of my knowledge, the gentleman looks puzzled.

"Funny, I was under the impression that she survived into her nineties."

"No, no, it's a common fallacy to think of her as an old woman; she definitely died in her twenties."

"Well, it's strange, because I was only reading about her yesterday and it definitely said......"

"Look, I am a bookseller, I should know."

Erudite conversation has never been my strong point. When the dust has settled, it turns out he was talking about Florence Nightingale, while I was talking about Mrs Beeton: a simple enough misunderstanding.

For the gentleman to return the books to his Tesco's carrier bag and storm out of the shop is, I feel, an over-reaction on his part. I call after him down the street.

"I can offer you £30 for Florence Nightingale." (It is lucky for me that a member of the vice squad is not within earshot.)

He is obviously not a proud man: he is back in the shop almost before I have finished the sentence.

"£30 for the book signed by the lady who lived to a particularly old age?"

"That's the one," I confirm.

As he reaches into his bag, I am seized by doubt. I am suddenly overwhelmed by an image of hundreds of lemmings leaping into the sea: Sam is clearly visible in the middle of them. I draw back from the cliff edge.

"I shall, of course, have to verify the signature first."

When I approach James' bookshop later that afternoon, I am carrying both the Mrs Beetons and the Florence Nightingale. The £30 is still safely in my pocket.

With a look of some disdain, James opens the more presentable Mrs Beeton and pulls out a slice of dessicated onion that has clearly not seen the light of day for the last sixty years.

"It's enough to bring tears to your eyes," he jests, before collapsing on the floor amid gales of uncontrollable laughter. By anybody else's standards, it is a fairly pathetic joke. By James' standards, it is clearly the best joke he has made in his life.

He gives me £20 for the two Mrs Beetons and turns his attention towards Florence Nightingale's signature.

"Ah, a genuine Florence Nightingale signature," he confirms.

The grin on my face spreads from ear to ear.

"Written, if I am not mistaken, by one of the lesser known Florence Nightingales."

The grin now belongs to James and is even wider than the grin that has disappeared from my face.

"You mean, it's not the 'lady with the lamp' Florence Nightingale, famous for her bravery in the Crimean War, who lived to ninety, and whose signature would be worth a small fortune."

"No, this is the Florence Nightingale who works part-time in a Bexhill Oxfam shop, lives in a bungalow, has three grown-up children, and whose signature is only worth something when it's written on a cheque."

I do not think James has enjoyed himself so much for years. He is clearly delighted by the effect his words are having on me.

I am disappointed in myself; I really should have been more concerned by the fact that the signature was written in biro.

Mostly, though, I am disappointed in Florence Nightingale. I really do feel that people with famous names should be more circumspect about where they write their signatures. It would be a fine thing if everyone, who happened to be christened Bill Shakespeare, went round writing 'William Shakespeare was here' inside the cover of every book they could lay their hands on. I, for one, would be in a perpetual state of over excitement.

It is some minutes before I come to my senses, and I find that, without realising it, I have entered into a bout of subconscious silent haggling. At least, I am haggling silently; James is totally ignoring me.

I am determined to spend my £30 and, whatever the price of the books that I pull from the shelves, I continue to throw hopeful glances in James' direction.

James clearly has no previous experience of silent haggling.

"If you've only got £30 to spend, why have you spent the last three quarters of an hour looking at a book marked £75?" (Michael would not speak to me in that tone; he would take my money.)

James is now plainly irritated by the duration of my visit. He reaches under his desk and produces two dilapidated leather volumes.

"If you give me £30 for these, I'm sure Nick Bernstein will give you a profit on them."

If he physically kicked me out of the door, he could not make his message any clearer. I have annoyed him to such an extent that he is providing not only the books, but also the method by which I can sell them.

I do not need a second invitation; I hand over my £30, pick up the books and return to my own shop. In the till, I find three pound coins, an old threepenny bit, and a note from Nick Bernstein saying he has called and will be back in six weeks time.

I open the first of the two volumes and somewhat dubiously examine the title page -

'The History of the Helvetic Confederacy'.

2 Volumes.

J.Plante. London 1800.

James has provided the books, but his proposed method of selling them is clearly going to be of no use to me whatsoever.

All I need to do now is find someone whose passion in book collecting is the history of Switzerland.

I locate my copy of 'Secondhand Booksellers in Europe' and open it at the appropriate section.

How do you say 'offers considered' in whatever language it is that they speak in Switzerland?

Tuesday 6th November

Cliches are brilliant things. They enable you to make really profound statements without actually having to think them up yourself. 'It never rains but it pours' may not qualify as one of the more profound cliches, but for two reasons it is appropriate to my present situation.

Firstly, it is appropriate because it is raining outside and, when customers come in saying, 'its raining cats and dogs' (that's not what I call a particularly profound cliche), I am able to reply, 'it never rains but it pours'. The customer can then leave the shop thinking what a pleasant and intelligent conversation they have just had.

Secondly, it is appropriate because, having just bought 'The History of the Helvetic Confederacy' for £30, a man sells me the Charles Knight edition of Shakespeare (unsigned) in two volumes, again for £30. As I pay him I mutter, "it never rains but it pours", to which he replies, "Yeah, it's raining cats and dogs out there".

I spend all afternoon polishing the scuffed leather bindings until they are transformed into a truly imposing set of books. The tragedy of the situation is that, for every collector of dilapidated books on Swiss history, there are probably a thousand collectors of handsome leather bound sets of Shakespeare.

If my £30 was invested in the Shakespeare rather than the Swiss history, I could probably sell it immediately, and go to the Ardingly Winter Antiques Fair on Wednesday to reinvest the proceeds in another book.

'If at first you don't succeed, try, try and try again,' is another extremely profound cliche. It has no relevance to my present situation whatsoever. 'If at first you don't succeed, cheat,' is a variation on the cliche which offers me a clear way out of my dilemma.

"That's a terrible sentiment," is my wife's immediate and understandable reaction. "How would you like the children to hear you speak like that?"

"They taught me to say it," I reply.

One by one, I have already abandoned the rules with which I set out on this exercise. What is to stop me now going back to the last chapter and rewriting it from the moment at which James is becoming irritated with me? The new version might read-

> *'James is now plainly irritated by the duration of my visit.*
> *He reaches under his desk and produces a sawn-off shotgun.*
> *'Buzz off creep.'*
> *If he physically kicked me out of the door, he could not make his message any clearer. I return to my own shop to find a customer waiting to sell me a set of Shakespeare for £30'*

Difficult to believe perhaps, but all good exciting stuff. Nobody need know about the 'History of the Helvetic Confederacy'. My money would then be invested in a highly desirable set of Shakespeare, which I could probably sell today, rather than a pair of books that I'm probably going to be stuck with until the return of Nick Bernstein.

Even more significantly, if I could establish the principle of cheating as a legitimate tactic, I would be in a situation where there would be no restrictions on my actions whatsoever. Why, if things got really sticky, there would be nothing to stop me walking into the British Library and removing a couple of rare incunabula by stuffing them up by trouser leg. Why, there would be nothing in the rules that prohibited a bit of breaking and entering at the local vicarage in order to acquire a particularly valuable edition of the Bible.

My thoughts are moving in a dangerous direction, and it is probably only the appearance of my friend, Trevor, that saves me from a period of detention in one of Her Majesty's prisons at some point in the not too distant future.

Trevor collects books in the same way as some people take in stray cats. He takes pity on them and attempts to provide them with a better life. He is obviously enormously distressed at the sorry state of 'The History of the Helvetic Confederacy'. He picks them up and strokes them gently.

"Poor things; I'm sure with some care and attention they'd be a lovely set."

He checks the price and reaches into his pocket to find the required £45. He leaves a happy man. (I think this is one of those sentences that still has the same meaning when you turn it back to front: i.e., we are both happy men.)

I settle back in my armchair and think through the consequences of this episode. Firstly, I have had a narrow escape and from now on there must be at least one strict rule: *NO CRIMINAL ACTIVITY.*

Secondly, I can now set my alarm clock for 5.30 tomorrow morning, drive for 1½ hours, and walk round a freezing cold field looking at over-priced antiques in the hope of finding a book on which I can spend my £45.

Sheer unadulterated bliss.

Wednesday 7th November

Sheer unadulterated piss.

I queue for the Ardingly Winter Antiques Fair in the same frame of mind as I queue to watch Hastings Town play football; with the misplaced belief that this time will somehow be better than all the previous times.

In theory, antique dealers should have good books to sell; in theory, antique dealers should not have a clue what those books are worth; in theory, I should be able to buy a book for £45 and sell it for a substantial profit.

In theory, of course, an educated man should not be queueing outside an antiques fair at five to seven on a freezing cold November morning, in order to earn a living substantially below the poverty line.

From behind the perimeter fencing comes the smell of bacon cooking and the sound of tarpaulins being moved as the antique dealers uncover their stock. If the traditional definition of antique dealers is correct, then that stock should comprise entirely of goods that are more than 100 years old. If my own definition of antique dealers is correct, then that stock is identical to the stock of a back street junk shop, except for being about 100 times more expensive.

As if to compensate for this obscene overvaluation of their stock, antique dealers have developed their own unique language, 'antique speak', which acts like a truth drug. It is a language that has the effect of making them describe their stock at its true value.

At seven the gates open and, once inside, I inspect the stalls with something approaching tunnel vision. I am single minded in the pursuit of my £45 quarry and I'm sure, if I was offered a £100 book for £30, I would haggle until I got the price increased to £45. I have no early success and, although I don't yet know it, my day is about to be dominated by the ambiguities of 'antique speak'.

It is not long before I come across the first example of this now familiar linguistic aberration. I pick up an early railway map and enquire as to the asking price.

"Four fifty, Guv," comes the muttered reply through a mouthful of egg and bacon butty.

An antique fair 'virgin' would at this point hand over a five pound note, assuming the map was about to become his property. At £4.50, the map would be good value. The 'virgin' has yet to realise that good value at an antique fair is as rare as compassion in the Tory party. What the 'virgin' doesn't understand is that four fifty in 'antique speak' means £450. It is a never-ending source of hilarity among antique dealers when a 'virgin' agrees to buy an item priced at several hundred pounds, and then attempts to pay for his purchase with a five pound note.

"I had a right moron here this morning," is a typical snippet of antique dealer's conversation. The only real moron is, of course, the antique dealer.

Antique dealers are sufficiently thick-skinned to price their wares at 100 times more than their true value, but they seem genuinely embarrassed at having to say those prices out loud. No doubt 'antique speak' had its origins with dealers mumbling the price as quietly as possible, until it evolved into the refined linguistic technique it is today.

At the next stall, I discover a book of Birket Foster engravings, priced "One sixty, Guv"; about a hundred pounds more than I have in my pocket. I can translate 'antique speak' as if by second nature: the 'two seventy five' demanded for a collection of hunting books registers in my brain, without conscious effort, as £275. As an experienced antique fair groupie, I do not allow myself to register a reaction to the absurdity of this demand; inwardly, I throw up.

I hesitate on being asked 'eighteen fifty' for a handsome folio volume of Gilrays engravings, before realising that any prospective purchaser would receive very little change from £2,000. I pick up my empty rucksack and continue on my forlorn way. After four hours, and not a single purchase, even my placid temperament is beginning to show signs of fraying at the edges. At the end of a row of stalls, I find an elderly white haired lady whose stock includes a box of Catherine Cookson paperbacks. I console myself with the thought that, if I buy them, it will at least help me recoup some of the days expenses. I make my selection, calculate quickly that I would be willing to pay up to twelve pounds, and look the old lady straight in the eye.

"How much for these Catherine Cookson paperbacks?"

"That would be one fifty."

Everybody has a breaking point, and this is the point at which I reach mine. One hundred and fifty pounds for paperbacks is, even by an antique fairs inflated standards, grossly excessive. I fling the books back into the box in a display of uncontrolled fury.

"What are you, mentally defective or something? Just because you call yourself an antique dealer, you think you can fill your stall with absolute crap and still charge the earth for it. If these books were new in W.H.Smiths, they wouldn't cost half what you're charging for them. They should take you and all the other antique dealers, lock you in a lunatic asylum and throw away the key. That way you couldn't get out to rip off innocent members of the public."

The small, white haired lady is obviously somewhat taken aback by my outburst.

"I'm sorry if you feel that's too much. You can have them for a pound if you want. We're only trying to collect money for Guide Dogs for the Blind."

I decide to bluff my way out of trouble.

"A pound, that's much more like it; I'll take them."

I place the books hurridly in my rucksack, turn, and head for the nearest exit. I do not look back at the expression on the old lady's face.

Once safely inside my car, I bury my head between my knees and scream silently to myself. I have worked hard all morning, and all I have to show for my efforts is a collection of books, the profit on which (after expenses) would be insufficient to provide even a light snack for a sparrow. I decide to take a detour and drive back by a longer, more leisurely route.

I head in the direction of Seaford, to see if Mr and Mrs Crutch are still in business there. In the village of Wiversfield, I stop at the local pub for a coca-cola; the pub is called 'COCK INN'. As I sip my drink, my mood begins to lighten. The sun is beaming through the windows, an open fire is burning in the hearth. I am in Cock Inn, on the way to see Mr and Mrs Crutch. I begin to smile. Language really is a wonderful, wonderful thing.

Friday 9th November

The most surprising thing of all about secondhand bookselling is that anyone should want to do it in the first place. What sort of parents are they that encourage their offspring with the suggestion -

"Have you ever considered becoming a secondhand bookdealer when you grow up?"

Where are the schools that have secondhand bookselling on the list of careers that they recommend to their pupils?

Why become a bookdealer, when there is such a shortage of property speculators, television interviewers, media tycoons, prime ministers? (All of which are well paid, and none of which require any particular talents or qualifications.)

Why become a bookdealer, when, if the same techniques were employed selling secondhand cars, the rewards would be a thousand times greater?

And yet people do become bookdealers. For every bookdealer that plunges lemming-like into the sea, there are always two or three young lemmings jostling to take his place on the cliff edge.

Possibly they are motivated by the same sense of calling which persuades a monk to take a vow of poverty. Possibly they are motivated by the belief that one day they will devise a foolproof scheme for making money out of secondhand bookselling. If they do succeed, they will not be the first. There are, to my knowledge, already two such schemes in operation.

I discovered the first such scheme when I saw it advertised in 'Exchange and Mart' -

Interested in making money from secondhand books?
Send £4.50 for a copy of my book "The Foolproof Guide
to Making Money from Secondhand Bookselling".
Money refunded if not completely satisfied.

I sent off my postal order and waited expectantly. After a fortnight, and no sign of the book in the post, expectation changed to impatience. After a month, impatience changed to annoyance. After three months, annoyance became anger. It was not until six months had elapsed, that anger finally became realisation; I had been done.

There was, of course, no such book as 'The Foolproof Guide to Making Money from Secondhand Bookselling'. The foolproof method was indeed foolproof; it consisted of persuading people to send off money for a book which did not exist. The problem was the only person making money from it was the one who placed the advertisement in 'Exchange and Mart'. It is a method of bookselling that I call the *"SELLING A BOOK BEFORE IT IS WRITTEN TECHNIQUE"*.

The second such method is equally foolproof, and is known as the *"SELLING A BOOK BEFORE YOU BUY IT TECHNIQUE"*.

It is a technique that was developed by one of my own customers, and came about as a direct consequence of her being the meanest woman who ever lived. She operated as a bookdealer within the limitations of two strict rules:

1. Never pay more than 50p for a book.
2. Never buy a book until you have already sold it.

The first time she visited my shop, she approached my desk with a selection of books that she had extracted from my shelves.

"Would it be possible to reserve these books for a week?"

I acquiesced, and a week later she returned smiling contentedly.

"I've come to collect the copy of "The Modern Sanitary Engineer" that you so kindly reserved for me. I think you'll find it's 40p less trade discount. I can't use the others I'm afraid."

I spent the next half hour returning the unwanted books to the shelves. It was to be a pattern of behaviour that would repeat itself weekly for years to come. Each week she would reserve a quantity of books, go home, try to sell them over the phone, and return a week later to purchase any for which she had found a customer. Each week the number of books she asked to reserve grew steadily larger. Each week the number of books she managed to sell remained constant; one.

It was a standing joke among the secondhand booktrade that I was the only bookdealer in south east England to let her get away with it. I found that, once I had allowed it to start, I did not have the strength of character to put a stop to it.

When her visits did eventually stop, there was no prior warning. By this time, she was reserving more books than she was leaving on the shelves. As she approached my desk for the last time, it was quite an achievement on her part to actually find me behind the stacks of books that she had reserved the previous week.

"I'll just pay for my copy of 'The Foolproof Guide to Making Money from Selling Secondhand Cars'. It's 35p less trade discount. You can put the rest of the books back on the shelves."

And that was the last I saw of her. She left me with a pile of books that took me the best part of a week to reshelve, and a foolproof method of selling books, which I am, all these years later, about to make use of myself.

The book to which I am about to apply this foolproof method is already in my possession. It is called -

'The Royal Liverpool Golf Club' - Guy B. Farrar 1933.

It was brought in by a gentleman from Battle who is selling off his father's library, and who brings me a few books each Friday on his way to the local swimming pool.

He brings them to me because he trusts me to offer him a fair price. Putting your trust in me to pay a fair price is a little like putting your trust in Tommy Cooper to be good at magic. We both do the best we are capable of, but the results are not always what we hoped they might be.

What I offer is a fair percentage of my selling price. The problem is that my selling price may or may not accurately reflect the true value of the book. What Tommy Cooper is to conjuring, I am to book valuation. Very much hit and miss.

My normal method valuation is to ask myself the basic,

"What can I get for it?" (I then offer half.)

Today, I judge each prospective purchase by stricter criteria,

"Is it worth paying £45 for?"

Under normal circumstances, the answer would be a resounding no; but these are not normal circumstances. I decide it is an ideal opportunity to try out the "*SELLING A BOOK BEFORE YOU BUY IT TECHNIQUE,*" and I manage to persuade the gentleman to leave the book with me for further research.

By now the experiment is sweeping me along in its ever

increasing momentum. I pick up the phone and dial the number for Grant Books of Droitwich, who advertise for golf books in 'The Bookdealer'.

"I have a copy of 'The Royal Liverpool Golf Club', and I wonder if you could give me some idea how much you'd be prepared to offer for it?"

There is silence at the other end of the line. I am about to discover if there is such a thing as a foolproof scheme for making money from secondhand bookselling.

"I can normally offer at least £100, depending on condition."

Eureka, eureka.

I pack the book in about forty different layers of cardboard, and phone the owner of the book to make sure he is willing to part with it for £45.

He is genuinely surprised at how much I can offer. As a foolproof method of making money, the *SELLING A BOOK BEFORE YOU BUY IT TECHNIQUE*" clearly has a great deal to recommend it.

Tuesday 13th November

Having the prospect of £100 to spend has certainly opened up a new perspective on life for me. It has also confirmed what I have suspected all along; I am one of the nation's poor.

Up to now, this has always been an issue of some contention. According to the Labour Party, the poor are those who cannot afford satellite television and a timeshare apartment on the Costa Del Sol. According to the Conservative Party, the poor are those who live in cardboard boxes that are less than ⅞ths of a centimetre thick.

My new found wealth has provided me with a fresh insight into the debate. It has enabled me to construct a definition of the poor that will settle the confusion once and for all. According to my definition, the poor are all those people who think that £100 is a lot of money.

It is a definition that enables me to categorize other bookdealers on a scale of A to Z according to their wealth. Mr Crouch is unmistakably category A+. His response to my cheery - "I've got £100 to spend and, if you're lucky, I might just spend it with you." - is a reply that propels me forcibly back in the direction from which I came.

"That's very impressive, Clive; why don't you come back when you've got some real money to spend."

None of the other dealers that I approach are quite so resilient to the mention of £100. Their responses enable me to place them in categories that range lightly through the early part of the alphabet, and climax in a strong statistical clustering round the WXY's. Only when I come to Michael do I find an unmistakable case of category Z-. His response to my talk of £100 is instantaneous, and consists of a distressing loss of control, on his part, over certain of the more basic of his bodily functions. I make my excuses and leave his shop by the nearest exit.

There is, of course, a danger in this new found affluence. I could, at any moment, decide to cash in on my success and bring my experiment to an abrupt conclusion. My problem is that, being unaccustomed to such riches, I am not quite sure if £100 is actually sufficient to bring about a fundamental change in someone's lifestyle. I am totally out of touch with the cost of round the world cruises and holiday cottages in rural France. I decide to consult my wife.

"If we suddenly had £100 to spend, what would we do with it?"

"Chuck out the old tumble drier and buy a new one."

I ponder briefly the benefits of never again having to go to work and sit all morning in damp underwear. It seems an insufficient reward for abandoning such an imaginative and potentially lucrative adventure in mid stream.

I shall, of course, persevere. (My ancestors would be proud of me.) As soon as the cheque from Grant Books actually arrives, I shall endeavour to reinvest it as quickly as possible in another book. (Before the attraction of dry, warm underwear becomes simply too strong for me to resist.)

Friday 16th November

There is a fundamental contradiction that underlies all secondhand bookdealing. The people who possess good books are under no financial pressure whatsoever to dispose of them.

Each week my advert appears optimistically in the local paper -
BOOKS BOUGHT. FAIR PRICES PAID.

Someone who has spent a lifetime building up a collection of rare colour plate books on the life cycle of the dragonfly will not see it and react -

"Wow, what a great idea, why didn't I think of it before? I can sell my collection of rare dragonfly books and buy a new three piece suite."

People spend a lifetime building up a collection of rare books, because it is something they wish to possess, and not something they would wish to dispose of at the earliest available opportunity.

The people who respond to advertisements, such as mine, are precisely those people who would not recognise a good book if it fell on top of them from a great height and knocked them unconscious.

Their conversation on seeing my advert is easy to imagine-

"Ere Gladys, you know those paperbacks we've had in the garage for years; the ones we use to wipe our greasy hands on. There's a bloke in the paper wants to buy them."

A bookdealer's life is, in many ways, a tragic one. He is destined to spend his days trailing from one house to another, looking at boxes of books that would be rejected as unsaleable by even the most downmarket Oxfam shop.

And yet, he doesn't actually need to go. It is the simplest of tasks to ascertain over the phone whether the caller is likely to have any saleable books to dispose of. Were Gladys' husband (Arthur) to telephone, it would sound something like this -

RING, RING.

The conversation that followed would then sound something like this -

ARTHUR: I'm phoning about your advertisement.
I've got some books you can come and make an offer on.
BOOKDEALER: What sort of books are they?
ARTHUR: Just ordinary books.

BOOKDEALER: Are they on any particular subjects?

ARTHUR: No, they're just ordinary reading books.

BOOKDEALER: Are they by any particular authors?

ARTHUR: No, they're by lots of different authors.

If, at this point, the dealer were to apply the most basic law of secondhand bookselling, he would save himself a great deal of time and trouble. Law 1 of bookselling reads -

'IF A CUSTOMER CANNOT DESCRIBE HIS BOOKS OVER THE PHONE, THEN HE HASN'T GOT ANYTHING THAT'S WORTH BUYING.'

Arthur will, though, still receive a visit. The dealer will go, because he knows that, if he doesn't, he will spend the rest of the week worrying about what he might have missed. Arthur could just be the exception to the rule.

When the dealer makes his call, he will find that Arthur lives on the 21st floor of the local council tower block. The lift will be out of order and, when he eventually arrives, near to collapse, at Arthur's front door, he will be informed by the bulky figure of Gladys that the books are stored in a garage at ground level where Arthur is waiting to meet him.

At no point must the dealer lose his sense of dignity. His very reputation is at stake.

The dealer will eventually tell Arthur that he has no sale for this particular type of book. Pushed for an explanation, he will point out that there is really very little sale for books so thickly covered in grease stains that it's impossible to decipher whether they've been written by Barbara Cartland or the Marquis De Sade.

Arthur, having little dignity and no reputation at stake, will point out angrily that, if the dealer had said all this on the phone, they would both have been saved a lot of unnecessary effort. The dealer will leave, displaying no visible signs of disappointment, in the direction of the next futile call. Arthur will be left to make his ponderous way to the 21st floor, where Gladys waits impatiently to find out how much money he is bringing with him.

If the dealer happens to be in luck, the next call, however, may be one to which the second law of bookselling applies. Law 2 of bookselling reads -

'THE BEST BOOK COLLECTORS ARE DEAD ONES'

The phonecall that all bookdealers long for is the one that begins -

"I'm phoning to see if you'd care to buy my elderly aunt's library on the life cycle of the dragonfly. She died suddenly last week."

"I'm terribly sorry to hear that."

It is essential that the bookdealer expresses this sentiment in a clear, unwavering voice. (Not an easy task when, in all probability, it is spoken at the same time as the bookdealer is leaping upwards in a state of such excitement that he invariably cracks his head on the bookshop ceiling.)

When the dealer arrives at the aunt's house, it is inevitable that an army of relations will have been and removed any of the books which have taken their fancy. The consolation for the bookdealer is that relations, given the choice between an 18th century set of books on the dragonflies of the southern hemisphere and a collection of Readers Digest condensed novels, will choose the condensed novels every time.

This clears the way for the remaining books to be bought at a reasonable price, and for the deceased aunt's niece to express her surprise that anyone - "could possibly be interested in so many old books about dragonflies."

The tragedy for the secondhand booktrade is that, for every elderly book collector that dies, there are a thousand Arthurs who are very much alive and only too eager to pick up the phone. The impact of this imbalance on the psyche of the secondhand bookdealer is inevitably a negative one.

The bookdealer who buys the dragonfly books has done so after travelling many thousands of miles, doing battle with many hundreds of Arthurs, and he is unlikely, therefore, to be willing to dispose of them to the first customer who happens to walk in and offer him a quick profit.

Most dealers will, in fact, take them straight home and refuse to let them out of their sight. Law 3 of bookselling reads -

'THE BEST BOOKS THAT A BOOKDEALER ACQUIRES ARE UNLIKELY TO EVER BE OFFERED FOR SALE'

It is Law 3 of bookselling that causes me problems when I attempt to spend my £125. (The cheque from Grant Books has arrived and he has been extremely generous.)

My main tactic now is to mention the money to as many dealers as possible and wait to see what reaction it produces. I pop into the bookshop next door to James, despite the fact that it's owner, George, in my A to Z classification of bookdealers, is definitely a grade D or E. It is a real surprise, when he shows a positive response to news of my experiment by putting down his pipe and looking up from the book he is reading. (I have seen him do both these things in the past, but never before have I seen him do both at the same time.)

His interest may be intellectual rather than financial, but it is sufficient for him to produce an unusual collection of seventeenth century pamphlets from his drawer. I have no way of knowing whether they are worth buying for £125. I am, however, in the interest of maintaining the momentum of my experiment, willing to gamble that they might be.

It is at this moment that Law 3 of bookselling raises its ugly head.

"They're fascinating aren't they? They came from the library of a vicar who died last week. They're not for sale I'm afraid."

It is a situation that calls for some imaginative negotiation. I know, from experience, that the only way to persuade a dealer to part with books he wants to keep is to offer to swap them for books which are even more desirable.

Like all bookdealers, I have collected my own horde of books that are not for sale. Among them is a seven volume leather bound set of George Eliot, worth approximately £125. I decide it is time to cash in on my assets.

"Any chance of swapping the pamphlets for a set of George Eliot?"

I know George is interested, because he attempts to take his pipe from his mouth and put down his book, before realising that he has done both these things already.

"Could I have a couple of days to think about it?"

I have made George an offer that is either a very shrewd move on my part or a very stupid one.

I now have to spend the next few days hoping that he might accept my offer, while at the same time hoping that he might decide to turn it down.

Sunday 18th November

The next day is Sunday. Call me old fashioned if you like, but I am a firm believer in the idea that Sundays should be a day of worship. I am, therefore, able, for one day at least, to put the dilemma of the seventeenth century pamphlets firmly out of my mind.

I once knew a family that went to church so many times on a Sunday, they took a packed lunch with them in order to save themselves the trouble of having to come home between services. In comparison to my own relegous devotion, however, their attitude towards Sundays now seems positively flippant.

The difference between them and me is that while they worshipped at the church of God, I worship at the church of the football field.

This Sunday's morning service is an eagerly awaited clash between St Vincents (for whom my 11 year old son plays) and Saplings, in the Rother and District under eleven league. It is played at the church of the Harley Shute Recreation Ground.

The encounter starts quietly with a great deal of jockeying for position, but little or nothing in the way of real action. It is only when one of the St Vincents contingent is sent sprawling in the mud by a blatant body check, that events begin to take on an all too familiar pattern.

The victim of the body check is immediately on his feet and squaring up to his opponent.

"You come near me again and I'll break your leg."

"Yeah, you just try it."

The two combatants charge at each other, heads down, like a pair of demented elephants. As they do battle on the half-way line, they are joined by half a dozen from each club who leap on top of them with cries of "St Vincents forever" and "Saplings are the champions".

It is only the approach of the referee that restores some semblance of order to the proceedings.

"Er, excuse me Mums and Dads, if you'd care to take up your positions on the touchline, I think you'll find the boys are ready to start their match now."

Behind the referee stands a motley assortment of small, shivering footballers, who are watching the proceedings with extremely embarrassed expressions on their faces.

One by one their parents extricate themselves from their scrummage of entangled bodies, brush themselves down, and rearrange themselves according to team allegiance on opposite sides of the field.

Once the football match is under way, the behaviour of the boys is impeccable. At the slightest hint of physical contact, the players concerned apologise profusely to each other.

"I'm awfully sorry, I think I just brushed against your leg as I attempted to kick the ball."

"No, no, don't apologise, it was my fault entirely; I wasn't looking where I was going."

Above their heads, the voices of the parents continue to hurl insults at each other.

"I'm coming over there to sort you out at half-time."

"I'll be waiting."

When the half-time whistle blows, the boys slink off apologetically to find their refreshments. The parents move aggressively towards each other until they meet in pitch battle in the centre circle.

The referee sensibly decides to conclude the match on the adjacent pitch where St Vincents win 2-1, the deciding goal being scored in the last minute by their outside left Gareth.

At the end of the game, the boys shake hands warmly, wish each other a happy and successful season, and move away in various directions to retrieve the prostrate bodies of their parents.

In the car on the way home, Gareth asks his father if he managed to get a good view of his goal.

"Not particularly, son; the mother of the Saplings goalkeeper was sitting on my head at the time."

The afternoon service is an under thirteen match between Spartan Rangers (for whom my eldest son plays) and Langney. By this age group, the number of supporters has been dramatically reduced, and whatever misbehaviour they display off the field is mirrored by the misdemeanours of the players on the field. By the age of thirteen, the example of their parents is clearly beginning to have its effect.

By the time the boys get to play at under sixteen level, the only spectators are either brain damaged or dogs. The behaviour of the players is totally out of control, and a fair indication of how they will perform in twenty years time, when they take their places on the touchline as the next generation of under eleven football supporters.

After the under thirteen game, I arrive home bloodied and bruised, with an hour to spare until the evening service commences. At five o'clock, I will be able to rewind the video recorder and settle down to watch a replay of this afternoon's Everton v Tottenham match. The absolute priority for the next hour is to avoid any situation in which I might be told the match score in advance.

At 4.15, the door bell rings. I open the door and, without looking to see who is there, I shout at the top of my voice -

"Whatever you do, don't tell me the score."

I look up to see the rapidly retreating figures of a couple of Jehovahs Witnesses. I can hardly believe my eyes; I have managed to achieve something I had always believed was impossible.

At 4.30, my four year old son turns on the television at the exact moment the commentator is giving an update of the score. I stick my fingers in my ears and begin to sing -

"God save our gracious Queen.

God save our noble Queen."

It is a technique that has saved me in many similar situations in the past. As I sing, I reach out and turn off the television with the big toe of my right foot.

I calculate that, if I walk slowly to the paper shop to pick up my copy of the News of the World (for its in depth analysis of international affairs), it will be five o'clock exactly by the time I return.

It is not until I am at the head of the queue in the newsagents, paper in one hand, packet of mint imperials in the other, that I notice for the first time the sound of a television behind the counter.

"Welcome back to Goodison Park, where the game has just ended with the score......"

I really have no choice. I drop my intended purchases to the floor, stick my fingers in my ears, and begin to sing -

"God save our gracious Queen,
God save our noble Queen,
............."

After a stirring rendition of the first couple of verses of the national anthem, I pick up my paper and sweets, and hand over a pound to a puzzled proprietor.

"Sorry about that, I didn't want to know the score."

I don't think he has the faintest idea what I'm talking about. I turn and walk out of the shop, past a line of disbelieving customers, who stare after me wide eyed and open mouthed. Even I am sometimes surprised at the strangeness of my own behaviour.

The game turns out to be the most excruciatingly boring 0-0 draw. My time would have been better spent considering the wisdom of offering £125 for a collection of pamphlets worth £40.

Monday 19th November

On Monday morning, I pick up the phone each time it rings in a state of some consternation. By this time, I am terrified that George might decide to take me up on my offer. Bill from Dartford has been in and informed me that it is possible to pick up seventeenth century pamphlets in London for four or five pounds each. Sothebys, apparently, often have collections of about twenty pamphlets which can auction for less than £100. (George's collection numbers approximately six.) Mr Crouch then comes in and tells roughly the same story.

There can be no question that I have made a serious error of judgement. There can also be no question that I now have to accept the consequences of my misjudgement, however disastrous they may prove to be.

Soon after lunch, George walks into the shop holding a carrier bag. I resign myself to the inevitable.

"I've been giving your offer a good deal of thought, Clive."

From the tone of his voice, it is immediately obvious that my experiment is about to receive an enormous self inflicted setback.

"And I've decided I'd like to do a bit more research on the pamphlets before selling them."

I peer into the top of the carrier bag: it contains half a dozen bananas and a small cabbage.

"That's alright, I quite understand, George."

I manage not to look too happy; I also manage not to look too grief stricken. I would hate him to take pity on me and change his mind at this late stage.

Law 3 of bookselling, let me remind you, reads -

'THE BEST BOOKS THAT A BOOKDEALER ACQUIRES ARE UNLIKELY TO EVER BE OFFERED FOR SALE.'

The effect of Law 3 on George is such that he cannot bring himself to part with decent books, even when he is offered three times more for them than they're actually worth. Its effect on me is that it has enabled me to make a particularly stupid offer and yet still get away with it. Law 3 of bookselling is a law for which I have every reason to be extremely grateful.

I still have £125 to spend, and it is the memory of a letter I first saw some years ago that provides me with an idea as to how I might be able to spend it. I decide that memory is entitled to a place within the structure of my mantra. Knowledge, resourcefulness, adaptability, perseverance, patience, people, memory: K.R.A.P.P.P.M. The extra M does tend to lessen the impact of the original. I reject the alternative M.K.R.A.P.P.P., on the basis that it sounds too much like a good name for a Scottish pop group, and settle instead for K.R.A.M.P.P.P. I go round the house chanting it to myself -

"K.R.A.M.P.P.P, K.R.A.M.P.P.P."

"Try wiggling your toes about, that usually does the trick," shouts my ever helpful wife from the living room.

The letter that I now remember belongs to a lady I first visited about five years ago. She wanted to sell a collection of books that were French, leatherbound, large and, in all honesty, virtually unsaleable. I was about to make a more than generous offer of £30 when the lady spoke for the first time.

"You're not the first dealer I've had in to look at them."

I decided I had better look at them more closely: I was in competition now. I suppose they were, on reflection, leatherbound; I suppose they were, on reflection, very large. I was about to offer sixty pounds when the lady spoke again.

"In fact, you're the third dealer I've had in to look at them."

I moved the books closer to the window. Perhaps I had been a bit mean with my original estimates. They were, when you held them up to the light, very big books indeed. If one thing brings out the best in me it's competition.

"I can offer you a hundred pounds for them."

"That's marvellous news; the other dealers said they were only fit for the rubbish tip."

I came away from that house with a collection of French, leatherbound, large books, which are still for sale in my shop today. (Available at a generous discount if anyone takes the lot.) I also came away from that house with a reputation, in the eyes of the lady occupant, as probably the most honest person who ever lived.

From that day onwards, she treated me as a kind of unpaid financial guru. She brought to my shop a steady stream of articles that she had for sale and asked for my advice. I passed judgement on jewellery, small items of furniture, maps, engravings (none of which I knew the first thing about), and she listened intently to every word I said.

It is the memory of one of the more interesting of these articles that now suggests a way in which I might reinvest my £125. The article in question was a letter signed by Louis XVI of France. She first brought it into my shop about 2 years ago and asked me to sell it on her behalf. The only decent offer I could obtain, though, was £100, and she decided that this was not enough to persuade her to sell it.

A month ago, she returned to my shop, explained that her financial circumstances had deteriorated, and indicated that, if I could again obtain an offer in the region of £100, she would now be prepared to accept it.

A month ago, the prospect of trying to sell the letter in order to earn a minimal commission did not seem a particularly enticing one. A month ago, of course, I did not have £125 that I was eager to spend. A month ago, of course, I was not a convert to the *SELLING A BOOK BEFORE YOU BUY IT TECHNIQUE.*

It now occurs to me that a signed Louis XVI letter might offer me an ideal opportunity to profitably reinvest my money. I decide to investigate the possibility further.

I telephone John Wilson of Oxford (a recognised authority on signed letters) in order to seek his advice. Mr Wilson, it turns out, is unavailable, and I end up explaining the situation to his female assistant.

"I have a letter signed by Louis XVI."

"Ya, ya."

"Written in 1774. . . ."

"Ya, ya."

"To the mathematician Bernard Goudin."

"Ya, ya."

"I wondered if I sent it to Mr Wilson. . . ."

"Ya, ya."

"If he would make me an offer on it."

"Ya, ya."

By this time, I am not quite sure if I am talking to a human being or a particularly sophisticated make of answering machine. Assuming she is human, she has certainly made my A to Z classification of bookdealers totally obsolete. In order to fit her in, there would need to be at least another twenty letters in the alphabet in front of the letter A.

She assures me between "ya, ya's" that Mr Wilson will be back on Friday and, if I can get the letter to him by then, they will phone me up straightaway with an offer.

"Would that be possible?" she asks.

"Oh ya, ya," I assure her emphatically.

Friday 23rd November

I learn today, if I did not know it already, that I am not destined to become a world authority on the authenticity of famous signatures.

It is the lady assistant of John Wilson who phones me back as promised. If anything, she is even posher today than she was on Monday.

"I'm phoning about the Louis XVIth letter, ya?"

"Ya?"

"I have some bad news for you, ya?"

"Ya?"

"The signature is that of the King's Secretary, ya?"

"Ya?"

"And the letter is worthless, ya?"

"Ya?"

"I'll post it back to you, okay, ya?"

"Okay, ya."

It's episodes like this that make you despair of people. First, I come across a Florence Nightingale, who is totally unknown, whose signature is absolutely worthless, yet who insists on signing every scrap of paper she can get her hands on in order to trick the book trade into believing they were signed by the famous Florence Nightingale.

I then come across a King Louis XVIth, who is incredibly famous, whose signature is worth a small fortune, yet who is so idle he can't even be bothered to sign his own letters.

I would have thought that, apart from having to lift up his own knife and fork and wipe his own bottom, signing his own letters would be about the only strenuous activity demanded of a king. No wonder the French people got fed up with him and had him guillotined. If you ask me he deserved everything he got.

I telephone the letter's owner with the bad news.

"I'm afraid the letter was signed by the King's Secretary, ya?" (My wife tells me that even I'm starting to talk a bit posh now. I can't say I've noticed any signs of it myself.)

The lady is disappointed and clearly a little confused.

"So why did the London dealer offer £100 for it two years

ago?"

It is one of those questions to which there is no answer. Why did it take the Conservatives until yesterday to get rid of Mrs Thatcher? Why do the England cricket selectors persist in picking Wayne Larkins to open the innings? Why did a dealer, whose most prized autograph is that of Jeremy Beadle, suddenly believe he could make his fortune by selling old signatures?

"I think you'll find it was just one of those stupid things that people do, ya?"

Tuesday 27th November

I continue to mention my £125 to every bookdealer I come into contact with, but it is becoming increasingly apparent that I am beginning to irritate them. They immediately try to change the subject to something more interesting, like Margaret Thatcher's resignation, or the crisis in the Gulf.

My crisis is that I am unable to find a way to spend my money, and I am reluctantly coming to accept that the dreaded word "auction" will soon have to enter the vocabulary of my experiment.

I hate auctions. I hate boot sales, antiques fairs, futile calls in council estate tower blocks; but, when I eventually give up bookselling, what I shall most be pleased to leave behind are auctions.

The first thing I hate about auctions is that you have to go to the auction rooms three times before you're actually allowed to buy anything. Just imagine if buying pot noodles from Sainsbury's worked on the same principle. Firstly, you would have to go to the supermarket to see what flavour you fancied; secondly, you would have to go and bid more for your pot noodles than anyone else was prepared to pay; finally, on the third day, you'd actually be allowed to collect your pot noodles and take them home with you. You'd be so hungry by this time that you might even enjoy eating them.

The second thing I hate about auctions is that there is actually very little chance of buying any books when you do make the effort to attend. It is a fact that 99% of auction visits are doomed to failure.

80% of the time there is nothing worth buying anyway. The auctioneer's advert may make the books sound like the best library to be offered for sale in years, but 80% of the time they will be crap. 15% of the time there will be someone willing to pay more for the books than you, and 4% of the time you will find that, when you come to collect the books, someone will have got there before you and stolen all the best ones.

On only one visit in a hundred will a dealer find books that he would like to buy, and actually succeed in purchasing them. He will do so, only because there is no one else in the room that day who considers them worth buying, and no one in the room the next day who considers them worth stealing.

A year later, he will realise that the reason nobody else wanted them is because they are totally unsaleable, and will have to be sold at a fraction of what he paid for them in order to cut his losses. It hasn't, though, let me assure you, always been like this.

Old time dealers still talk about the 'good old days', when books at auction were plentiful, sold at £1 per lot regardless of what they were, and always went to the same dealer. If a first edition folio Shakespeare and a copy of the Gutenberg bible had turned up together in the same auction lot, the bidding would still automatically have stopped at £1. It was possible to go to the local auction rooms, spend £7.50, and come away with enough stock to keep your shop filled for the next twenty five years.

It was the arrival of my friend, Roy, in Hastings, that finally shattered this cosy arrangement in the local auction rooms. On his first visit to Harry Lucy's, he had successfully bid two pounds for a set of Morris's British Birds, when he was approached by a rather agitated elderly gentleman.

"I'm awfully sorry, but there seems to have been a misunder-standing."

"Misunderstanding?"

"Yes, you see we buy all the books in these auction rooms."

My friend Roy's reaction was to suggest to the old man, using the 1950's equivalent of the expression 'sod off', that he should go away. (I have checked with Roy, and apparently the 1950's equiva-lent of the expression 'sod off' was, in fact, 'sod off', and that is precisely what he told the old man to do.)

From that day on, bookbuying in the local auction rooms would never be quite the same again.

When I started bookselling, books at auction were still plenti-ful, but there was by now a healthy competition between the dealers wishing to acquire them. It was all very civilised; should £100 worth of books be offered for sale, the competition would be between the bookseller willing to pay ten pounds for them, and his rival who felt it would be incredibly irresponsible to pay more than £9.50. The successful bidder would still go home worrying -

"Oh no, what have I done? I've paid ten pounds for these books and I'm sure they're not going to price up at any more than £100."

Nowadays, competition for £100 worth of books would be between the bookseller willing to pay £99 for them, and his rival willing to go all the way to £99.50. The successful bidder would still go home rejoicing -

"That's marvellous, I've managed to buy £100 worth of books and I only had to pay £99.50."

It is into this cut throat world of modern day auctioneering, that I am about to have to enter in order to spend my money. Don't get me wrong, though; it is still possible to make money from auctions, but to do it you need to have certain qualities that I do not possess.

You can make money from auctions if you already have loads of money before you start. Mr Crouch recently went to auction willing to pay up to £3,000 for a sixteenth century book on China. He got carried away at the auction, paid £11,000 for it, and still managed to sell it the next day for £12,500 - to the collector who commissioned the underbidder. I could probably make money from auctions if I had that sort of money.

You can make money from auctions if you have expertise. Last year, an early Sherlock Holmes item turned up in the local auction room. Fifty dealers looked at the book, but only the dealer who bought it for £35 recognised it for what it was; a book he would be able to sell the next day for £3,000. I could probably make money from auctions if I had that sort of expertise.

You can make money from auctions if you are ruthless. There are dealers who go to the same auction each week and buy all the books regardless of what they cost. They lose money for a while, until all the other dealers get so pissed off they go away and attempt to buy their books elsewhere. From then on the first dealer gets all the books for next to nothing. I could probably make money from auctions if I was that ruthless.

Loads of money, expertise, ruthlessness; it is unfortunate, to say the least, that I do not have any of the qualities required to make money from buying books at auction. The quality that I do possess, and that points me in the direction of the auction room, is desperation: I am running out of alternative ways in which to spend my money.

I scan the local papers, make a list of auctions between now and Christmas, and prepare to do battle with dealers who possess, in abundance, all those qualities that I so sadly lack.

Tuesday 4th December

I spend the next week visiting every auction between Brighton and Folkestone; I do not manage to buy a single book. I do not fail because I am outmanoeuvred by dealers who are wealthier, wiser and more ruthless than I am. I fail because all the books on offer are crap. I have indeed seen a less craplike selection of objects coming out of the backside of a cow.

I console myself, between auctions, with a tour of the secondhand bookshops of south east England. My reception is everything I might have predicted. I am sure, if Salman Rushdie took a package holiday in Tehran, he would be met with less hostility than a stranger receives on entering a secondhand bookshop. Booksellers hate customers. Booksellers open bookshops because it enables them to indulge their passion for buying books, and because it offers the prospect of a tranquil life. Customers enter bookshops with the almost universal intention of disturbing that tranquility.

Certainly there are customers who spend twenty minutes in a bookshop, select as many books as it is possible to carry, pay for them in cash, and leave with a cheery - "See you next time I'm in Hastings."

Booksellers love such customers. Sadly for booksellers, customers such as this are few and far between. The customers that enter bookshops are far more likely to fall into one of the following categories -

- Armed robbers.
- Mothers asking if you have a toilet which their children can use.
- Children asking if you have a toilet which their mother can use.
- People sheltering from the rain.
- Shoplifters.
- Mental defectives wanting to know if you sell bananas.
- Customers who announce their arrival by saying, "I've brought the wrong glasses with me. I can't see a thing."
- Dealers looking for books marked at a quarter of their

true value.
- Husbands hiding from their wives.
- People collecting for charity. (There have been many
    days when I have had to give more money to charity
    than I have made from selling books.)
- People with half an hour to kill until their bus arrives.
- People wanting to put a poster in your window.
- Wives looking to see where their husbands are hiding.
- Lonely old age pensioners who just want someone to
    talk to. (I tell them to piss off.)

It is little wonder that the look that greets me when I enter a bookshop for the first time is more one of trepidation than exultation. My own appearance probably categorises me somewhere between a potential armed robber and a mental defective. I am sure, if I walked unexpectedly into my own shop, I would be strongly tempted to throw myself straight out again.

I once visited a recently opened Eastbourne bookshop, that I only reached after an hour long walk from the railway station. As soon as I pushed at the shop door in order to get in, I noticed the owner of the shop pushing the glass door in the opposite direction, in an attempt to keep me out.

"Would it be possible to come in and have a look
    around?" (Push, push.)
"What sort of books are you interested in?" (Push, push.)
"Oh, just books in general." (Push, push.)
"We don't have a section for general books, so go away."
    (Push, push, slam.)

It is a technique for keeping out undesirables that most bookshops employ with a greater or lesser degree of subtlety. Possibly the least subtle of booksellers in this respect is Sam; Sam hates customers more than any other bookseller I know.

It is a tradition among Bexhill booksellers to assume that all customers are shoplifters. Sam's immediate predecessor in Bexhill would have followed her own grandmother round the shop, in the firm belief that she was nicking all the best books by stuffing them in her inside coat pocket. Sam would solve the problem by refusing to let his grandmother into the shop in the first place.

It is a common occurrence to arrive at "Sam's Emporium" (in

reality a garage in a Bexhill side street), to find a rope across the entrance and a notice attached which reads -

'THIS SHOP IS NOW FULL SO EVERYONE ELSE GO AWAY'

A motley assortment of customers will be hovering outside on the pavement, staring into the shop, where Sam will be clearly visible, drinking tea, and most definitely alone.

Once allowed inside the shop, customers are subjected to a running commentary from Sam as to exactly what it is about them that he so despises.

"Bloody customers, I hate them; bloody time wasters everyone. They only come in because its pouring with rain and their bus isn't due for another half an hour. If they do see a book they fancy, they nick the bloody thing."

It is an interesting reflection on human nature that, despite his almost unique approach to customer relations, Sam runs the busiest bookshop on the south coast.

He is no less unkind to customers selling things to him. I was once in Sam's crowded shop, when a very respectable elderly gentleman asked Sam nervously if he was interested in buying old videos. The gentleman spoke in the faintest of whispers, and approached Sam in the darkest corner of the shop. Sam replied in the loudest of voices, and held the videos above his head for everyone to see.

"You disgusting old man.These are absolutely filthy. What's an old pervert like you doing trying to sell films called 'Sex orgies through the ages'? You should be absolutely ashamed of yourself. Don't you agree everyone?"

By this time the gentleman had abandoned the videos and was fleeing in the general direction of Beachy Head; in all probability never to be seen again.

Sam's methods may be extreme, but there is a little bit of Sam in every bookdealer.

When Roy had a bookshop in Battle, his method of deterring customers was simple. He allowed customers into his shop, and then refused to sell them anything. His stock was the finest in the region, and remained so, for the very simple reason that he was never prepared to part with any of it. The shelves were crammed with mouthwatering volumes, none of them priced, and none of them for sale. Should a customer object and enquire as to exactly which books in the shop were for sale, Roy would point them in the direction of a shelf of Mills and Boon paperbacks, just inside the door, and tell them to take their pick.

All booksellers, to some extent, are reluctant to part with their stock. Even my mother-in-law, who has worked for me for less than six months, is beginning to show marked tendencies in that direction.

A customer recently spent all morning in my shop, before discovering a book he had wanted for years buried under a pile of National Geographic magazines. He brought it triumphantly to the desk and handed it over to my mother-in-law. Her reaction confirmed that she has all the qualities necessary to make a first rate bookseller.

"I can't sell you this I'm afraid. I quite fancy reading it myself."

It's amazing how even the dullest book can seem interesting when somebody else is about to buy it.

In the course of the week, I visit bookshops of all shapes and sizes; from the bookselling equivalent of the humble parish church, to the St. Pauls Cathedral of secondhand bookshops - Howes of Hastings. The staff at Howes sit in raised pulpits, and gaze down on their congregation with looks of such disdain, you feel you have to buy something just to get out of the shop with your dignity intact.

I pay £15 for a nineteenth century travel book on Scotland, rub out the price as soon as I get back to my shop, and put it on my shelves marked £12. I consider it a small price to pay for the pleasure of browsing through their magnificent stock.

In the course of the week I have travelled about 500 miles, and at no point have I come even remotely close to spending my £125. I sink into the comfort of my armchair and wait to see what happens next.

What happens next is that the phone rings. It is Ian from Maidstone. "I've got another collection of railway books. You interested in buying them if I bring them down Friday?"

"How much do you want for them?"

"About ninety quid I should think."
"Any chance of finding a few more books and making it
  £125?"
"I'm sure that could be arranged."
"I'll take them then."

Friday 7th December

It is not, I think, widely known, but it is a fact, that when J.R.Hartley began his search for a copy of his own book 'Fly Fishing', the first bookshop that he telephoned was mine.

"I'm looking for a copy of Fly Fishing by J.R.Hartley," came the now familiar request.

"Is that Hartley spelt L-E-Y?"

"That's it."

"Never heard of it, mate" was my considered reply.

I did, in fact, have three copies of the book in stock, but it is a strict rule of mine never to encourage anyone who is searching for a specific book. (It has been on my conscience ever since, that if I had been a bit more co-operative, we would all have been spared those nauseating commercials.)

The explanation behind my refusal to help booksearchers is as follows:-

1) I did not become a bookseller in order to spend all day hunting through my shelves for books which, in all probability, aren't there anyway.

2) On the few occasions when I have succeeded in locating a particular book for a customer, it has invariably turned out to have the wrong coloured dust jacket or to be too expensive at 45p.

3) Booksearchers, in my experience, do not actually want to find the books they are looking for; they enjoy searching for them too much. I'm sure the greatest pleasure in J.R.Hartley's life was annoying busy bookdealers with his incessant phone calls. I'm sure his greatest disappointment was when he eventually bought a copy of 'Fly Fishing' and found it was exactly the same as when he wrote it; pure drivel.

If the prize for most annoying booksearcher in the world must go to J.R.Hartley, there can be no doubt that second prize would go to one of my customers. The second most annoying booksearcher in the world bursts into my bookshop at exactly the same moment as Ian from Maidstone is leaving it. The second most annoying booksearcher in the world is more usually called by his other title: 'Pain in the Arse'.

Ian from Maidstone has been true to his word, and has delivered three box-loads of railway books as promised. He has also been true to the lemming-like nature of booksellers and decided that he now wants £150 for them. I manage to knock him down to £125 by a) pointing out that I only have £125 to spend, and b) promising him first refusal on any decent books that I buy in the future.

I have just closed the lid on the final box when 'Pain in the Arse' enters. I really should have been expecting him, he hasn't been in for the last forty five minutes.

"Got any books on railways?"

"No, nothing I'm afraid."

"What about in that box there?"

He points to the middle of the three boxes. I sit on it.

"No, just rubbish I'm afraid."

"What's in that box?"

He points to the second box. I lift up both my legs and place them forcibly on top of it.

"More rubbish I'm afraid."

"What's in there then?"

He motions towards the final box. I lean backwards until my head is resting on top of it.

"Rubbish, more rubbish."

Even as I lie across the top of the three cardboard boxes, 'Pain in the Arse' is beginning to pull at a slight opening which he has discovered at the side of one of them.

"I think this book's got something to do with railways."

I crane my neck to one side; it would be pointless to argue with him. Clearly visible, through the ever-widening aperture, is the dustjacket of a book, on which is written *'RAILWAYS, RAILWAYS, RAILWAYS - EVERYTHING YOU EVER WANTED TO KNOW ABOUT RAILWAYS'*

"I'd forgotten about that one," I confess.

'Pain in the Arse' manages to extricate it from it's position, despite the fact that my entire body weight is bearing down upon it. As I sink slowly nearer the floor, I realise that I am beginning to lose control of the situation.

'Pain in the Arse' continues to wrench railway books from the cardboard boxes and, each time he does so, he announces, "and another one," before tossing it backwards over his shoulder.

Each time he does so, I murmur apologetically, "I'd forgotten about that one," and sink a little further towards the ground.

After approximately half an hour, the floor of the shop is strewn with dilapidated train books, and the body of a secondhand bookseller lying motionless on top of three squashed and empty cardboard boxes.

I look up just as 'Pain in the Arse' is about to leave my shop.

"Not quite what I'm looking for I'm afraid. Not that I've got any money on me anyway."

As he walks past the window, he sticks his thumb in the air and grins at me broadly. I lift my left leg about six inches off the floor and wave pathetically back.

About two hours later, I have recovered sufficiently to repack the books and start out on a journey to Hythe. As I drive along, I consider how bookselling never ceases to amaze me. Ian, who is a dealer, bought the books off a dealer, sold them to me, a dealer, and I am now on my way to sell them to another dealer. If someone could explain mathematically how we all manage to make money out of them, I'm sure they would be well on their way to a mathematical explanation of the nature of the universe.

My original intention had been to telephone a specialist railway dealer and offer him the books as a single collection. On Tuesday, however, a bookseller from the Old Gallery Bookshop, Hythe, came to my shop and expressed his disappointment that I did not have any railway books in stock. I told him about the collection arriving Friday and offered to take them to Hythe for him to look at.

"Only if it's not out of your way," he commented.

"Not at all" I replied, as if I am in the habit of driving eighty miles just to sell a few old books.

In the interests of my experiment, I am now spending so much time driving through the roads of Kent and Sussex, that locals are standing at their gates and waving to me like an old friend.

The books, in all honesty, are a major disappointment. In the life cycle of a secondhand bookdealer, Ian is clearly hovering dangerously close to the cliff edge. I am more than a little embarrassed when the Hythe bookseller asks how much I want for them.

"200"

"How much?"

"200"

He doesn't speak.

"And if you take them, I'll give you first refusal on any decent books I buy in the future."

"It's a deal."

I drive home, a £200 cheque in my pocket, waving warmly to the locals as I go.

Thursday 13th December

The more money I have to spend, the more difficult it becomes to spend it. I decide it is time to leave my familiar territory behind me and head in the direction of the London auction rooms. At 7.19 on a freezing December morning, I join the queue of tired-eyed commuters and board the Charing Cross train. As my fellow travellers unfurl their morning papers, I pull a crumpled sheet of paper from my jacket pocket and begin to read. On it, a writer friend, Chris, has scribbled some advice on the literary merit of my experiment. (I am in awe of Chris. He once had a comedy script rejected by the B.B.C.) His advice is,

(1) Not enough danger.

(2) Not enough sex.

It will be an hour and a half before the train arrives in London. I decide it is an ideal opportunity to do something about his criticisms. While the train is stationary at Battle, I purchase a British Rail cheese roll from the mobile buffet, and by Robertsbridge I have eaten it. I cross danger off the list with a satisfied grin. (I would have used a pencil, but it's broken.)

At Stonegate, I lean back and stare straight up the skirt of the girl sitting opposite me. I would have been quite happy looking up her skirt all the way to London, but her legs don't go that far. (She does, in fact, get off at Tonbridge.) I cross sex off the list with a lecherous grin (I haven't been able to borrow another pencil).

If ever this diary is published, the benefits of Chris' advice to any accompanying publicity campaign would be enormous. I close my eyes and allow my thoughts to wander.....

......*"Reflections From a Bookshop Window" is a blockbuster. Danger on a train, sex on a train; a sure fire hit for book lovers and train enthusiasts everywhere. Buy it today.....*

I sleep all the way between Sevenoaks and Waterloo; all this danger and sex has fairly worn me out. I get off at Charing Cross and walk to Hardwick Street, where I somewhat apprehensively enter the rooms of the Bloomsbury Book Auction.

In theory, I might be able to spend my £200 in Bloomsbury; in practice, I will have to outbid the likes of Maggs and Quaritch in order to do so. (For me to bid against Maggs and Quaritch is the equivalent of Accrington Stanley having to play Liverpool and Manchester United one after the other on the same day.)

You can tell a great deal about bookshops from the people they employ; Maggs and Quaritch are represented at the sale by two attractive young ladies in long flowery dresses. I grin at them in a way intended to convey the message "Better watch out - Mr Big's in town". They glare back at me as they might at something the cat's puked up. Perhaps one day I'll be able to employ attractive young girls in long flowery dresses. For the time being I shall have to make do with a distinctly overweight mother-in-law.

What I need is a plan of attack. I abandon any attempt to view several thousand books in under an hour, and begin to jot down some rules of engagement on the back of my catalogue.

1) Only bid for very old books.
2) Only bid for very big books.
3) Only bid for books with lots of pictures in them.
4) Only bid when the ladies from Maggs and Quaritch are in the toilet.

When the auction begins, the ladies from Maggs and Quaritch spend more time in the lavatory than they do in the saleroom; they are, though, never absent at the same time. I am beginning to worry that there might not, in fact, be room for both of them to be in the lavatory at the same time, when they rise together, fling back their hair theatrically, and squeeze side by side through the toilet door.

I focus on the auctioneer's voice....

"Lot 79. Francis Grose. 'The Military Antiquities of England' in two volumes. Who'll start me at thirty?"

I check my catalogue; they're certainly big; they're certainly old; and they've got lots of pictures in them. I raise my hand above my head and leave it there. (I am not asking for permission to join the ladies in the lavatory. I am, in fact, bidding.)

"35, 40, 45, 50, 55, 60, 65, 70....the bidding is with the ... er ... bearded gentleman on my right. Anymore..? Anymore..? Sold for £70, and that is Mr...?"

"Linklater"

"Link...water?"

"Linklater"

My voice comes out in something of a high-pitched squeal. It may not have quite the ring of a Maggs or a Quaritch, but everyone has to start somewhere. The ladies re-emerge simultaneously from the lavatory. (I'm beginning to have my doubts about those two.) I wink at them mischieviously; they glare back at me in a way that suggests they consider me deficient in some of my more basic faculties.

About an hour later, I take advantage of their renewed absence to purchase 'Gothic Ornaments in the Cathedral Church of York' by J.Halfpenny, and midway through the afternoon session, I acquire 3 volumes of 'The Old Northern Runic Monuments of Scandinavia and England'. The only runic monument I know is my mother-in-law, but I buy them because they are old, illustrated, and so enormous that, when I eventually pick them up, my spinal column collapses.

I hurriedly calculate that I now have £35 left to spend. I tear up my rules of engagement and proceed to bid up to £35 for every lot that is offered for sale. (I sense the auctioneer is not amused when I drop out of the bidding at £35 on a collection of Gentlemans magazines that eventually sells for £7,000.)

When the last lot of the auction (No.578) is reached, I still have £35 to spend. The book on offer is 'The Shooters Guide' by B.Thomas. When the bidding reaches £35, the auctioneer looks automatically in my direction. I raise my hand more in hope than expectation.

"35...the bidding is with the persistent gentleman on my right. Anymore...? Anymore...? 40...the bidding is with the lady in the front row. Anymore...? Anymore...? Sold to Quaritch for £40".

The auctioneer raps his hammer down sharply and announces the end of the sale. The young lady in the front row turns in my direction and, if I'm not mistaken, winks at me in a distinctly mischievous manner.

Friday 14th December

Booksellers hate Christmas. Booksellers hate winter when it's too cold for customers to come into freezing secondhand bookshops. Booksellers hate summer when it's too hot for customers to come into stuffy secondhand bookshops. Mostly, though, booksellers hate Christmas.

Just as other shops are becoming busier and busier, secondhand bookshops become emptier and emptier the nearer you get to Christmas Day. It is a sad fact of bookselling life that people do not, as a rule, give secondhand books for Christmas presents.

The exception to the rule is me. Everyone who receives a present from me knows exactly what to expect under the wrapping paper. My children would be absolutely horrified if they woke to find anything other than a selection of secondhand books waiting for them on Christmas morning.

They like to pretend otherwise. This year they played a great trick on me and handed me a Christmas list which read simply,

"ANYTHING AT ALL EXCEPT SECONDHAND BOOKS".

It's a good job I knew they were only joking. I still remember the pleasure that last year's offering gave to my eldest son, Stephen. I took his gift, and in an elaborate wheeze, I placed it first in a box that once contained a computer, then in a box that once contained a portable TV, before constructing around it a parcel that gave every indication of containing a BMX bike. His mounting excitement as he unravelled his present was a pleasure to behold.

"I've got a feeling it's going to be a bike."

"No, no. It's going to be a .... television."

"No, no. It's going to be a .... computer."

"No, no. It's a ..... 1972 edition of the Guiness Book of Records. Er....thanks a lot, Dad".

He contained himself as best he could before the tears of gratitude came flooding out. He wept all the way to his bedroom where he remained with his book for the rest of Christmas Day. (I didn't realise when I bought it that it would prove to be such an absorbing read.)

I really do feel that more people should give secondhand books as Christmas presents. I spread my Bloomsbury purchases across my desk. There are books here that would make a wonderful Christmas present for someone. I can visualise the scene in that lucky person's living room on Christmas morning. . . .

WIFE: (unwrapping her present) "Oh darling, a Janet Raeger negligee and a bottle of Yves Saint Laurent perfume. You really are too generous."

HUSBAND: (unwrapping his present) "Oh darling, 'The Old Northern Runic Monuments of Scandinavia and England' in three volumes. You shouldn't have." (He attempts to lift them up and, as he does so, he puts his back out so badly he has to spend the rest of the holiday in traction.)

My normal idea of decorating the shop for Christmas is to stick a sign in the window which reads 'CLOSED TILL NEXT WEEK'.

This year I decide to make an exception. I enthusiastically decorate the shop with something like a thousand paper chains, and place in the window an enormous sign which reads,

'SECONDHAND BOOKS
THE IDEAL CHRISTMAS PRESENT'

I remove all the old volumes from my window display and replace them with my Bloomsbury purchases. I then return to my armchair and wait expectantly.

After about ten minutes, Dick, who has recently opened a bookshop about three doors down the road, fights his way through the paper chains and approaches my desk.

"I'll take the 'Military Antiquities of England' in two volumes please, Clive."

"A little something for the wife at Christmas, eh Dick?"

"Er, no . . . actually she's asked for some bath salts and a box of initialled handkerchiefs."

Bill from Dartford then comes in and purchases 'The Old Northern Runic Monuments of Scandinavia and England'. He looks at me somewhat strangely when I ask if he intends to give them to a relative as a surprise Christmas present.

"No, I can't say I'd planned to," he explains as he makes what seems like an unnecessarily hasty exit.

I am beginning to wonder if all my decorating has been in vain. I step out onto the pavement in order to assess the impact of what remains of my Christmas window display. Beneath my notice -

'SECONDHAND BOOKS
THE IDEAL CHRISTMAS PRESENT'
- lies a single, somewhat lonely-looking volume.

I hastily calculate that there are still eight more shopping days till Christmas. I shall leave the book in the window and wait to see what happens.

Somebody, somewhere, would be thrilled to receive 'Gothic Ornaments in the Cathedral Church of York' as a Christmas present. My problem is that that somebody is probably 250 miles away in York, and highly unlikely to be walking past my window within the next eight days.

We shall see.

Saturday 15th December

Technically, I still have another £35 to spend. I have also developed a seemingly insatiable appetite for setting out on long and potentially futile journeys. At 8.30 on a Saturday morning, when any normal bookseller would be going back to bed after a hearty breakfast, I find myself walking across London in the general direction of Farringdon Road. I stop to ask a policeman if I'm going the right way for the book market.

"You are. But I wouldn't go on a Saturday if I were you," he replies.

Farringdon Road is part of our bookselling heritage. There have been secondhand bookstalls in Farringdon Road for longer than any bookdealer that I know can remember. Indeed, Farringdon Road is so much a part of our bookselling folklore, that I had always taken it for granted it had long since ceased to exist.

On Thursday, in the Bloomsbury lunch break, I went in search of a chip shop and stumbled across the remnants of the Farringdon Road bookmarket. I asked the proprietor when he puts out new stock.

"Saturday, but you don't want to come then."

I asked friends if it was still possible to pick up bargains there. (In the old days, you could apparently fill a suitcase with rare books and still get change from half a crown.)

"Only on Saturday, but you don't want to go then."

I felt like someone invited to a party in a haunted house. By the time I arrive at this particular party, the other guests are already in position and waiting for the festivities to begin.

The bookmarket consists of four tarpaulin covered tables, surrounded by some of the meanest looking people I have seen since I last took part in a Butlin's 'Ugliest Man of the Week' competition. I squeeze amongst them and wait.

As a newcomer, I have no idea of what will happen next. I decide to watch my neighbour and copy every move he makes. For the first half hour, my neighbour doesn't move a muscle; nobody moves a muscle; I don't move a muscle.

At one minute to nine, my neighbour begins to snort like a

pig; everybody begins to snort like a pig; approximately five seconds later, I begin to snort like a pig. At nine o'clock, at exactly the moment at which the tarpaulin is pulled from over the books, my neighbour hurls himself into the air and comes crashing down upon the table. At nine o'clock, all the customers hurl themselves into the air and come crashing down on the table. Approximately five seconds later, I hurl myself into the air and come crashing down on the table.

By the time I arrive at the table, approximately five seconds behind everybody else, it is empty. As bookmarkets go, it's a bookmarket that is over unusually quickly. As I lay disbelieving across the top of an empty trestle table, the regulars move away to examine piles of books almost bigger than they are.

A book, the title of which translates into 'The Clock in Art', comes flying in my direction with the comment, "I don't want that. It's not in English." It strikes me behind my left ear. I pull it towards me like a baby.

As I hand over £2 for my book, the proprietor recognises me and comments,

"You shouldn't have come on a Saturday; I did warn you."

"I won't again. Don't worry."

Saturday 22nd December

A week is a long time in secondhand bookselling.

I have always thought it would be nice to write a sentence that would become really famous. I have a feeling that *'a week is a long time in secondhand bookselling'* might become a really famous sentence. I know sentences that aren't any better than that which have become really famous.

In years to come, on television quiz shows, they might ask, "Who first said *'A week is a long time in secondhand bookselling'?*" And if I'm watching, I'll be able to answer, "It was me." I always try and answer the questions when I'm watching television quiz shows. It would be nice to get one right for a change.

The best thing about the sentence *'A week is a long time in secondhand bookselling'* is that it's true: a week is a long time in secondhand bookselling. (I always argue that if you think up a really good sentence, you should make sure you use it at every conceivable opportunity.)

A week ago, as I walked down Farringdon Road with my copy of 'The Clock in Art', there was no doubt in my mind that my first visit to Farringdon Road bookmarket would be my last. A week though, as the saying goes, is a long time in secondhand bookselling. (I'm still not sure I'm using this sentence as often as I should.)

Shortly before nine o'clock, I take my place among the 'Phantom of the Opera' lookalikes that make up the clientele of the Farringdon bookmarket. I still have £35 to spend, and I now believe I have the necessary expertise that will enable me to spend it. I have thought about little else for a week (and that's a long time in secondhand bookselling). I am determined that this time I will not be beaten.

There are two main differences that persuade me that this week I can succeed. The first main difference is that this week I have a plan. At one minute to nine, I put that plan into action. At exactly the moment when everybody snorts like a pig, I snort like a pig. At nine o'clock, at exactly the moment at which the proprietor begins to tug at the tarpaulin, I hurl myself into the air and prepare to come crashing down upon the table. A week of planning has gone into the timing of this prodigious leap.

It is somewhere between the hurling and the crashing that it dawns on me that I have leapt too early. It is apparent by looking beneath me as I fly through the air, that it will not be onto the books that I will be crashing, but onto the tarpaulin which is still being dragged across the top of them.

By the time the other customers have decided to hurl themselves into the air and come crashing down upon the table, I am lying on a tarpaulin in a Farringdon Road gutter. If this was television, there would be a cigar for me to smoke and a pianist playing the music from the Hamlet advert. If this was a dream, I could wake up and say, "Thank God it was all just a terrible dream."

I am, however, very much awake, and I am being approached by a small figure staggering under a pile of books that are several times his own body weight. It is my eleven year old son, Simon.

"I've managed to get a few books for you, Dad," he explains.

The second main difference between this week and last is that this week I have brought one of my children to assist in my efforts.

My instructions to him were crystal clear -

"Watch what I do and do the same."

He watched as I snorted like a pig, and five seconds later, he snorted like a pig. He watched as I hurled myself into the air, and approximately five seconds later, he hurled himself into the air and came crashing down upon the table. His timing was better than mine; by the time he arrived at the table, the tarpaulin was gone and lying crumpled underneath his father in the gutter.

His timing was indeed perfect; he arrived at the books before the regulars, who were delayed watching the unusual tactics of a newcomer who had flung himself at the table while the tarpaulin was still on top of it. For a few brief seconds he had the bookstall to himself. He carries his selection towards me and places it beside me in the gutter.

"I'm proud of you, son," I exclaim.

The books he lays beside me consist of a run of Roy of the Rover annuals and a selection of Roald Dahl paperbacks. I do not allow even the slightest flicker of disappointment to register on my face.

"Exactly the ones I would have chosen, son."

I pay for them, and search among the books that no one else has wanted in a desperate attempt to finally get rid of the rest of my money. I purchase four antiquarian books, for no other reason than their total prices add up to £35, and walk away from Farringdon Road for what will definitely be the last time.

"Are we going anywhere next week, Dad?" enquires my ever eager business partner.

"Who can tell what we'll be doing, son. A week's a long time in secondhand bookselling."

Thursday 27th December

After two days of eating and watching television, I decide it is time for some fresh air. I leave my boys in their bedrooms, still reading this year's Christmas presents, and shut the front door behind me. I am about to set off down the road when my wife calls after me.

"You've forgotten your hat, darling."

The check cap she extends towards me is this year's Christmas present from her to me. It is so small that, if it belonged to the man with the tiniest head in the world, it would still be tight fitting: it offers my amply proportioned head about as much protection as one of Twiggy's bras would offer to Dolly Parton's tits. I thank her for reminding me, and balance it precariously on the top of my head.

Even strangers are unable to refrain from commenting "Great hat" as I walk towards town. James takes one look as I enter his shop and remarks "No need to ask what you got for Christmas." If I did not know my wife better, I might suspect that this is some kind of revenge for the 'Wisdens Cricketers Almanak' I gave her as a present last year.

While I am in James' shop, a lady dealer from London comes in and enquires about a volume of World War I poetry that James recently had in his window. James informs the lady that he sold it to Robert at Croft books, and she goes rushing off in the direction of the High Street. A few minutes later, the same lady comes hurrying in the opposite direction (Robert apparently having sold the book to Michael), before she returns, approximately half an hour later, to find the book clearly displayed in the window of the bookshop next door to James. (Michael apparently having sold the book to George.)

The sight of the lady dealer carrying away the volume of World War I poetry in the direction of London (where no doubt it will pass through the hands of half the capital's book dealers) raises in my mind one of the two great philosophical questions that so dominate the conversation of serious minded booksellers. (There are, to my knowledge, two serious minded secondhand booksellers, and they both live on the Isle of Wight.) The questions that so concern them are:

1) Where does space end up? It can't just go on forever; there must be a point at which space doesn't go any further.

2) Where do secondhand books end up? Books cannot simply move forever through the booktrade becoming more and more expensive. There must come a point when they are so expensive that there isn't a dealer in the country who can afford to buy them.

Two theories have been put forward as possible solutions to this apparently insoluble second problem. The first theory was widely accepted about twenty years ago, and is still officially recognised by the A.B.A. It is known as - 'THE THEORY OF THE IMPLODING BOOKSHOP'.

The theory states - "a book shall continue moving through the secondhand booktrade, increasing in price as it goes, until it reaches a shop where the stock is so expensive that it can move no further. The book will then be joined by such a vast quantity of other over priced books, that the shop will collapse inwards under the weight of its own stock. That shop will be said to have 'imploded', and will cease to exist. Its place will then be taken by the next most expensive bookshop, which, after a given length of time, will in turn 'implode'."

It is a theory (alternatively known as the big bang theory) which, twenty years ago, appeared to offer a plausible explanation as to the ultimate reality of the secondhand booktrade. It has, though, since been superceded by something known as - 'THE THEORY OF THE BLACK HOLE BOOKSHOP'.

It was the discovery by Driffield of a previously unknown bookshop in a remote district of Ireland, that first alerted the secondhand booktrade to the possibilities of this alternative. The shop he discovered is known as the 'Black Hole Bookshop'. It was apparently set up by the Irish Government under a business initiative scheme, in order to bring much needed employment to a depressed part of the country. The shop buys expensive books, and then sells them back to the booktrade at a tiny fraction of what they have paid for them. The shop loses vast sums of money, but provides a much needed source of employment for the local population.

Its existence leads to a theory which reads - "a book shall move through the secondhand booktrade, getting more expensive as it goes, until it is purchased by the 'Black Hole Bookshop'. It will then be sold back to the booktrade at a price that will enable it to start out once more on a return journey to the 'Black Hole Bookshop'. This process will then continue indefinitely."

The implication of this theory is that the entire secondhand booktrade is financed by the Irish Government.

At this particular moment, it would help my experiment greatly if I could make direct contact with the 'Black Hole Bookshop'. I have already got my money back on my Bloomsbury purchases, but to make a profit on my £200, I now need to sell 'Gothic Ornaments in the Cathedral Church of York' and the antiquarian books I bought in Farringdon Road. The local booktrade are showing a marked reluctance to help them on their way to Ireland.

I attempt to call Driffield, but his phone has been disconnected: I telephone directory enquiries, but they have no number listed under 'Black Hole Bookshop'. In desperation, I turn to James -

"Is there really a 'Black Hole Bookshop', James?"

"Of course there is, Clive."

"I thought there must be."

"And there's a man called Father Christmas."

"Well, I know that, James."

Friday 4th January

My new year resolutions are -

1) Visit the dentist regularly.

2) Never, never, never, buy another copy of the 'Gothic Ornaments in the Cathedral Church of York'.

The Farringdon antiquarian books have been disposed of (by letting them go for less than I paid for them), but 'Gothic Ornaments' lies buried in my window under a blanket of fallen paper chains, and beneath a notice which reads -

"SECONDHAND BOOKS.
THE IDEAL CHRISTMAS PRESENT"

I feel the fact that there are now more than 300 shopping days left till next Christmas has somewhat taken the edge off this particular advertising campaign. I replace it with a notice which reads -

"JANUARY SALE.
MASSIVE REDUCTIONS"

No sooner have I done so, than a lady, straining under the burden of approximately twenty four laden carrier bags, enters the shop in a state of some excitement and enquires eagerly.

"Anything on Prince Charles in the sale?"

"Nothing, I'm afraid."

"Anything on the Queen Mother?"

"Nothing, I'm afraid."

"Anything on any member of the royal family?"

"Nothing at all, I'm afraid."

"Well, what subjects have you got books on then?"

"Ornament."

"Ornament?"

"Gothic ornament."

"Gothic ornament?"

"In the Cathedral Church of York."

"Gothic Ornament in the Cathedral Church of York?"

"You've heard of it then? It's that large dilapidated book in the window. It's very cheap."

"It would bloody well need to be. Blimey, I've been to better book sales in xyz's."

With that, she picks up her twenty four carrier bags and sweeps out of the shop, trampling on fallen Christmas decorations as she goes. I have received many criticisms in my bookselling career, but never before have I been unfavourably compared to a xyz booksale. It is the ultimate professional insult.

A xyz booksale consists of the most boring books published in the course of the year, reduced by approximately five pence a volume. They then spend so much advertising it on TV, that people travel miles just to discover what a load of crap it all is.

I decide to cheer myself up with a tour of other people's January sales. Tony Neville's half price sale in Rye might, on the surface, appear to be the ideal destination. The only problem is that the prices he halves are about four times what I would charge for the same books. His sale offers me the opportunity to buy books at approximately double the price I'd sell them for. The 'Black Hole Bookshop' could buy well there, but I can't. I head for Michael's.

Michael has spent so much advertising this year's sale that Coca Cola's advertising budget looks stingy in comparison. His books are so cheap that, if they got any cheaper, he'd actually be paying his customers to take them away; and yet, when I enter his shop, he is alone and studying a book entitled 'The Joys of Bankruptcy'. I realise immediately I have not come to the right place to be cheered up. I head for Sam's, despite the fact that Michael attaches himself to the back of my jacket, and hangs there pleading with me to come back and spend some money in his shop.

Sam is another one who's beginning to worry me. There can be no doubt that he is becoming more and more eccentric. He is now almost totally obsessed with finding new ways of stopping customers getting into his shop. Two weeks ago, the notice outside his establishment read - '*ADMITTANCE BY INVITATION ONLY*'. (Sam obviously has pretensions to be the 'Stringfellows' of secondhand bookshops.) Last week, the notice had been changed to one which read - '*THE PUBLIC LIBRARY IS JUST ROUND THE CORNER SO GO THERE INSTEAD*'. This week's notice, despite making no reference whatsoever to January sales, has still managed to attract a queue of customers which stretches halfway down Parkhurst Road. The message that so attracts them is simplicity itself: it reads - 'SOD OFF'.

There really is no justice. I'm sure if 'Gothic Ornaments' belonged to Sam, he'd have customers tearing each other limb from limb, simply to be allowed to touch it. The solution to my problem is suddenly and blindingly obvious. I enter 'Sam's Emporium' and approach the proprietor.

"Want to buy a book, Sam? It's going cheap."

"It's a bit like a budgie then," retorts Sam, before collapsing amid torrents of laughter.

Whatever it is that makes Sam so successful, it clearly isn't his sense of humour.

Thursday 10th January

When I attempt to deliver 'Gothic Ornaments' to Sam, the sign outside his emporium reads - *'ADMITTANCE FOR FREE-MASONS AND MEMBERS OF MENSA ONLY'*. Sam is nowhere to be seen. According to Jean, Sam turned up for work, read the notice, and, assuming it applied to him as well, went straight back home.

In a last desperate attempt to dispose of 'Gothic Ornaments' before this afternoon's Bloomsbury auction, I head for the Old Town. The notice on James' window reads *'RING BELL FOR ATTENTION'*: the notice on James' bell reads *'OUT OF ORDER'*. George has already packed up and gone home at a time when most milkmen are still only halfway through their morning deliveries; and the only shop to which I can gain access is Roberts.

Robert is interested. He actually takes £25 from the till and is about to hand it over, when he hesitates, and reveals exactly why it is that he is affectionately recognised as the Eeyore of the secondhand book trade.

"I really don't know if I should. I might never sell it."

"Of course you would," I assure him, as I reach out and attempt to snatch the money from his grasp.

"No, I've changed my mind. I don't want it."

"Not even for fifteen?"

"No."

"Ten?"

"No."

I would be quite happy to carry on and sell it for a couple of quid, but it is obvious that Eeyore has made up his mind and will not be budged. I sometimes think that, if Robert was offered Audubons birds for a fiver, he'd turn it down in the belief that the market for rare colour plate natural history books might collapse the next day. I return 'Gothic Ornaments' to my bag and head towards the railway station.

I decide that, if I am going to London, I might as well take 'Gothic Ornaments' with me and try to sell it in the bookshops of Charing Cross Road.

The booksellers of Charing Cross Road are not in the least bit interested. They are not even interested enough to take a look at it. Only in Henry Pordes do they get me to take the book out of the bag. The proprietor then takes one look at the book, one look at me, and comes to the not unreasonable conclusion that I have probably just nicked it from one of the other shops in the road.

I do not understand why, but even being suspected of shoplifting turns my face bright red and has me rushing from the shop in a decidedly guilty manner.

I deposit 'Gothic Ornaments' in a left luggage locker at Charing Cross Station, and take the tube to Bloomsbury. During the journey I make a list of the books on which I spent my last £200, and beside each entry I write the amount for which I sold it. Beside 'Gothic Ornaments in the Cathedral Church of York', I write 'UNSOLD'. I then add up the figures to discover exactly how much money I now have available to reinvest at Bloomsbury.

I do not think the total thus revealed will make me a leading contender for any 'Businessman of the Month' award. It is not a total that could in any way be described as an 'outstanding achievement'. It is a total which can, in fact, be adequately described by one word only; the word is 'pathetic'. The total is £225.

For a month I have travelled repeatedly to London. I have suffered damage to my spine in a Bloomsbury auction room, damage to my pride in a Farringdon gutter, damage to my dignity in a Charing Cross bookshop, and all I have to show for it is a measly £25 profit. If I did not realise it already, then this is the moment at which I am finally forced to accept that I will never be headhunted by Quaritches. I enter Bloomsbury Book Auctions and prepare to start all over again.

The Charing Cross dealers, who were not even prepared to glance at my own offering, have now travelled to Bloomsbury, where they seem willing to practically kill each other for the right to buy books which appear no better than 'Gothic Ornaments', but which are decidedly more expensive.

Any attempt on my part to join the bidding is hindered by the fact that, each time I prepare to raise my hand, it feels as if the entire weight of 'Gothic Ornaments in the Cathedral Church of York' is bearing down upon it. I eventually find the strength to bid

£225 for some Turner plate books - that finally sell for £500 - before resigning myself to the fact that this really isn't an auction at which I would be wise to spend my money.

I resist the temptation to abandon 'Gothic Ornaments' in the Charing Cross left luggage office, and take my place on the Hastings-bound train. As the commuters around me open Evening Standards and Dick Francis novels, I pull out 'Gothic Ornaments in the Cathedral Church of York' and begin to read. The more closely I study it, the more puzzled I become as to what it was that persuaded me to buy it in the first place.

When I eventually get back to my shop, I place 'Gothic Ornaments' in the position for so long occupied by the 'British Friesian Herd Book Vol.39'. I am sure there are members of the local wildlife that will find it an excellent home. I trust they'll be happy there.

Friday 25th January

If I had to give advice to a young man considering becoming a secondhand bookseller, my advice would be "DON'T DO IT". If I had to give advice to a secondhand bookseller considering writing a diary of a year in bookdealing, my advice would be "CHOOSE A YEAR IN WHICH THERE IS UNLIKELY TO BE A MAJOR WAR".

It is proving difficult to motivate myself in the pursuit of books, while the nation is glued to its television screens watching an aerial bombardment of Iraq and Kuwait. It is proving difficult to make whimsical observations about the world of secondhand bookdealing, when everyday conversation is dominated by talk of Scud missiles and Armaggedon.

I continue, though, to go through the motions. I now have £240 to spend (Dick has bought 'Gothic Ornaments' for £15, and leaves the shop with the comment, "I never could resist a bargain"), and I travel to Brighton, Lewes, Tunbridge Wells and Ardingly Winter Fair in an attempt to spend it. The only purchase I make that gives me any satisfaction whatsoever is a bacon roll at Ardingly.

I continue, of course, to make my rounds of the local bookshops. I discover there are now so many notices in front of Sam's Emporium, that there are more people outside reading the notices, than there are customers inside looking at books. Many people, it seems, come to read the notices and then head straight back home again.

Today's addition to the display reads:-

SOME OF THE THINGS WE DO NOT SELL

TADPOLES
FORD CAPRIS
SWIMMING POOLS
CUP FINAL TICKETS
BOOTHS GIN
CEMENT
RACE HORSES

CAST IRON BATHS
SNOWBALLS
MARS BARS
ACORNS
CHRISTMAS PUDDINGS
TORNADOS

Inside, Jean is scurrying round the shop in the firm belief that anyone wearing a coat or carrying a bag must, by definition, be a book thief. I do not think she will relax until Sam makes it a rule that only customers stripped to their underwear can enter the shop. (That might not be such a bad idea; I'd be there every day.)

My own attitude towards book thieves is far more laid back. My feelings towards them are more ones of pity than of anger. A recently published opinion poll asked the public who they considered the most stupid people in the country to be. The results were as follows:-

1) Members of the Conservative Party Think Tank
2) Quiz show hosts
3) The England cricket selectors.

Without for one moment wishing to challenge the supreme position so rightly given to the gentlemen who devised the Poll Tax as a fair system of taxation, I am surprised by the absence of any mention of secondhand bookthieves. I have never ceased to wonder at the mentality of a shoplifter, who walks past jewellery shops and hi-fi stores in order to steal from a secondhand bookshop.

My complacent attitude towards shoplifters was developed over many years. It came about because, when I started in business, I was the only cheap secondhand bookshop in the area. It was possible for shoplifters to remove books from my stock, but it was impossible for them to find anywhere to re-sell them. Should I notice books had gone missing, I only had to be patient and, sure enough, a couple of days later, the thief would invariably turn up and try to sell them back to me. Shoplifters seemed to operate under the not unreasonable assumption that I had so many books in my shop, I would never realise I was being asked to buy my own books back again.

My method of punishing shoplifters was simple; I shouted at

them extremely loudly. In my experience, they would run a mile and never come back again. I outlined the method to Sam.

"You are sure it works aren't you?"

"Absolutely positive," I assured him.

A week later, two young men in leather jackets approached Sam's desk and demanded the money from his till. Sam took one step backwards and yelled at them at the top of his voice,

"Go away, you spineless wimps."

The reaction of the spineless wimps was to tie Sam to his chair and walk out of the shop with his day's takings.

I later suggested to Sam that he probably hadn't shouted loudly enough. Sam then proceeded to demonstrate exactly how loudly he was capable of shouting. Some people never appreciate good advice.

Over the years, I managed to whittle away at the number of shoplifters until they were no more than a minor irritation. It was only when I employed my mother-in-law that things began to go wrong. I started to have my doubts when I discovered I had less money at the end of each week than I had at the beginning. I arrived at the shop unexpectedly one afternoon, to discover it was so full of previously banned shoplifters, that it was almost impossible for me to push my way through the front door.

Even the fact that every single customer was wearing an overcoat bursting at the seams (it was a hot summer's day), and carrying a couple of bulging suitcases, had failed to arouse the slightest hint of suspicion in my mother-in-law's brain.

"But they all look such nice people", she insisted, when I pointed out the possible implications of this bizarre coincidence.

To make matters worse, it later transpired that one of these shoplifters had managed to devise a 'FOOLPROOF METHOD FOR STEALING FROM SECONDHAND BOOKSHOPS', which he had been operating in the St.Leonards area with considerable success.

It was a row of science fiction paperbacks in Peter White's recently opened shop that first alerted me to this particular 'FOOLPROOF METHOD'.

The significance of these books is that they were the same books that I had bought from a regular supplier the day before, and which I had assumed were still unsold in the paperback section of my shop.

By comparing notes, we calculated that the man who sold me these books on Monday had somehow managed to sell them again to Peter on Tuesday.

His method was indeed foolproof, and operated according to the following timetable:-

MONDAY	Sells me a collection of science fiction paperbacks.
TUESDAY	1) Brings me a second collection of science fiction paperbacks.
	2) While I am assessing them, goes in the next room and steals back the books he had sold me the day before.
	3) Sells these to Peter White and steals back the books he had sold him on Monday.
	4) Heads for Michael's.
WEDNESDAY	Sells me a collection of science fiction paperbacks.....

His method meant that he was able to empty his bag and fill it up again in every shop he entered. The logic of this method, if my calculations are correct, is that after a week he must have been selling me the same books that I had bought from him a week before.

If his method hadn't cost me such a substantial amount of money, it would be difficult not to feel a sneaking admiration for the man's ingenuity.

When he next appeared in my shop, I confronted him with the news that I had uncovered his 'FOOLPROOF METHOD'.

"Good isn't it," came his guilt-ridden reply.

Monday 28th January

It is an established part of auction mythology that it is possible to unintentionally purchase an item simply by sticking your finger in your ear at an inappropriate moment. Dealers may dismiss this suggestion as laughable, but their behaviour at auction would seem to indicate that it is a threat they take very seriously indeed.

Dealers not actually bidding for a particular lot stand with hands clasped behind their backs in a state of communal rigor mortis. Only between lots do they take the opportunity to clean the inside of their ears, scratch their bums and pick bogies from their noses. Between lots, it would be difficult, in fact, to find a dealer who doesn't have a finger operating in one or other of his bodily orifices. The moment bidding on the next lot begins, however, and an absolute stillness descends once more on the auction room.

The nervousness of dealers is a consequence of the seemingly infinite variety of bidding techniques which they employ. There are as many styles of bidding as there are dealers. Imagine any contortion that the human body is capable of performing, and somewhere in the country there will be a dealer who uses it as a method of bidding. Flutter an eyelid or wiggle an ear while the auctioneer is looking, and it might just cost you a substantial sum of money. As soon as the bidding for Lot 1 at today's Hambrook sale begins, I place both hands on the seat of my chair and sit on them.

I have come to Hambrook because it fits in with my newly devised campaign plan, and despite the fact that I am in the middle of a particularly nasty bout of influenza.

I have decided that the main obstacle to my spending £240 at auction is the presence of other dealers. The other dealers are there because they have seen the auction advertised, and I have therefore decided to concentrate my energies on auctions for which there has been no advertising. Only when I attempt to find such an auction, do I discover it is a plan that is fundamentally flawed. If other dealers can't find out about a sale, then how can I be expected to? I decide to concentrate, instead, on auctions for which there has been very little advertising indeed.

The only advertisement I can find for today's sale is tucked away at the bottom of a page in the 'Antiques Trade Gazette'. I make sure no one else is looking while I study it, and then take the added precaution of stuffing the paper down the back of the settee. I arrive fully expecting to be the only dealer present, and find instead a saleroom more packed than a sardine salesman's conference.

Lot 1 consists of three volumes of Whittakers Alamanak. The auctioneer, by his own admission, is inexperienced in handling books, and attempts to get the bidding started at £200. They eventually sell for £1, and only achieve that figure because someone in the audience manages to mistime a particularly nasty facial spasm. I may be unkind, but I do feel that someone with an almost total lack of control over their facial muscles would be well advised to steer clear of auction rooms. I have barely had time to blow my nose when the bidding for Lot 2 begins.

The lot in which I have decided to reinvest my £240 is No.29 (a gallery of original engravings), and I therefore have time to mentally rehearse the bidding style that I intend to employ today. It is a style which I would classify as 'SUPERCOOL', and consists of an almost imperceptible nodding motion of my head.

After Lot 27, I scratch my bottom vigorously; after Lot 28, I once more blow my nose; and by the time the bidding for Lot 29 begins, I consider myself fully prepared. When the bidding reaches ninety pounds, I enter the competition with a gentle raising and lowering of my head.

"Ninety"

"One hundred"

My immediate rival has a bidding style which I would classify as 'SUPERSUPERCOOL'. It is a basic 'SUPERCOOL' technique of gently raising one of his fingers, but is made 'SUPERSUPERCOOL' by the fact that, each time he bids, he raises a different finger from the time before. The auctioneer thus has to carry out a quick check on each of the gentleman's fingers in order to ascertain whether he is bidding or not.

I tilt my head backwards, and I am about to lower it, when I become aware of an almost unbearable tickling sensation on the inside of my nose.

"Aaahhhchooo"

"Is that a bid, sir?"

I nod my head to confirm it as such.

"One hundred and ten"

"One twenty"

As soon as I raise my head, the tickling sensation returns.

"Aaahhhchooo"

"One thirty"

"One fourty"

"Aaahhhchooo"

My sneezes are coming with great regularity and perfect timing. I decide to allow nature to do my bidding for me.

"One fifty"

"One sixty"

"Aaahhhchooo"

"One seventy"

At this point, 'SUPERSUPERCOOL' drops out of the bidding; either he has run out of money or he has run out of fingers. He is probably unwilling to use the same finger more than once in case people think of him as merely 'SUPERCOOL'. His method is one which must place severe restrictions on how much he can spend on any one auction lot.

He is replaced in the bidding by a woman sitting in the front row who employs a technique that comes from the 'MENTALLY DEFECTIVE' school of auction bidding. Her technique consists of sitting in a kind of scrunched up ball, before suddenly leaping skywards in an explosion of flailing limbs, while at the same time screaming at the top of her voice,

"......Yeeeeeees"

The dealers sitting near her topple from their chairs in a state of severe shock, and it is all the auctioneer can do to prevent himself falling headlong from his rostrum.

"One eighty"

As soon as the people in the front row regain their chairs, and the auctioneer is sufficiently composed to look in my direction, I prepare to bid. Nothing happens. The reflexive nature of my sneezing has clearly been inhibited by the violent nature of the lady's bidding. I sense a murmur of disappointment move through the room. All eyes are fixed in my direction: I decide to imitate nature.

"Aaahhhchooo"

"One ninety"

Attention switches to the lady in the front row. People sitting near her cling grimly to the framework of their chairs; the auctioneer places his hand across the top of his glass of orange juice, and the lady in question scrunches herself up into a tenser and ever-tighter ball.

"......Yeeeeeees"

All attempts at damage limitation are proved to be in vain. The same people fall from the same chairs; orange juice erupts upwards through the auctioneer's fingers, and the auctioneer himself is only held in position by the restraining hands of his female assistant.

"Two hundred"

"Aaahhhchooo"

"Two ten"

"......Yeeeeeees"

"Two twenty"

"Aaahhhchooo"

"Two thirty"

"......Yeeeeeees"

"Two forty"

I shake my head slowly from side to side, cross No.29 from my catalogue, and resign myself reluctantly to the fact that there is nothing in the sale in which I can reinvest my money.

It is some minutes before I pay any attention to the bidding and, when I do so, I find that it is continuing to spiral upwards in pursuit of the same volume of engravings. (It is spiralling upwards in more senses than one; the same lady is still involved in the bidding.)

"Eight hundred"

"......Yeeeeeees"

By this time a voluntary exclusion zone has come into existence within a ten metre radius of the lady's chair; former occupants of this area having retired to a safe distance. The orange juice has been forcibly expelled from the auctioneer's now empty glass, and the auctioneer has got down from his rostrum in order to conduct proceedings from ground level.

"Eight fifty"

"Nine hundred"

"......Yeeeeeees"

"Nine fifty"

There comes a point where bidding for a lot reaches such a high figure that dealers focus on the competition with feelings of curiosity and admiration. There does, though, come a point where the bidding is so ludicrously high that those reactions disintegrate into ones of ridicule and mockery. That point has long been passed with respect to Lot No. 29.

It is now clear that someone is about to pay over nine hundred pounds for a book which is worth, at most, four hundred. Dealers smile at each other, safe in the knowledge that it is not going to be them who will be handing over the money for Lot 29.

"One thousand pounds"

"......Yeeeeeees"

"One thousand one hundred"

The elderly gentleman who has forced the bidding up to this point, by means of a severe facial twitch, turns his back on the auctioneer and enters the lavatory, twitching merrily as he goes.

"One thousand one hundred. The bidding is with the lady sitting alone in the front row. Anymore.... anymore.... ?"

The eyes of the auctioneer scan from one side of the room to the other. Dealers fix their gaze on a point between their shoes and hold their breath.

"One thousand one hundred. For the last time. One thousand one hundred. Going, going...."

"Aaahhhchooo"

I had contained myself for as long as possible, but eventually the renewed tickling sensation in my nostrils had become more than a man could bear. It could prove to be the most expensive sneeze in history.

"One thousand two hundred"

"The bidding is back with the bearded gentleman. Any more..?"

".......Yeeeeeees"

"One thousand three hundred"

The auctioneer looks immediately in my direction, but I am already running out of the main door in the direction of Hambrook High Street. I am on the pavement outside when the next sneeze arrives.

"Aaahhhchooo"

Behind me, I can just make out the auctioneer's voice calling after me.

"Are you still bidding, sir?"

"No, I'm bloody not," I mutter to myself as I continue running. I do not stop until I am approached by a couple of medical-looking gentlemen in white coats, who enquire if I know the way to the Hambrook auction rooms.

Wednesday 6th February

James has a big one, but not as big as George's. The biggest one in the old town, though, belongs to Robert. It is so big that Robert still believes that this is the reason he has acquired the nickname Eeyore. Michael has quite a big one, especially when you consider that he hasn't been doing it long. He does, though, have the rather disconcerting habit of taking it out and showing it to everybody who comes into his shop. Sam had one once, but, according to his wife Jean, it is such a long time since he used it that it is now covered in cobwebs and of no practical use to anyone. Mr Crouch has an enormous one, but while he is happy to talk about it on the telephone, he has never allowed anyone to see it. Dick claims that his one is bigger than Mr Crouch's, but no one believes him.

Mine may be small, but I have always believed that size isn't that important anyway: it's what you do with it that counts. My reference library does in fact consist of one volume only. It is a reference library that would be considered unimpressive if it belonged to the local greengrocer. For a practising secondhand bookdealer, it is a reference library that can only be described as hopelessly inadequate. My reference library comprises of a single copy of Book Auction Records. Not only is my reference library somewhat on the small side, it is also somewhat outdated. My reference library comprises of a copy of Book Auction Records for the year 1903.

The lack of quality in my reference library doesn't prevent me from using it extensively. Whenever somebody offers to sell me a decent book, I always make a great show of looking it up in Book Auction Records. Whatever information I find there, then becomes a key element in the bargaining process.

"A copy of this book sold at Sothebys for £3, but I can offer you £30."

My customer then goes away thinking they have received ten times more than they would have got for the book at Sothebys. At no point do I mention that it was over 85 years ago that the book auctioned for £3.

Wherever I go looking for books, Book Auction Records

1903 goes with me. In a Bexhill antique shop this morning, I discover 2 volumes of Paynes Dresden Gallery on sale for £30. I hurry to my car to look them up; they sold in 1903 for 15/-. I turn them down on the basis that £30 is probably all that they're worth.

In the afternoon, James phones me up and tells me he has picked up a marvellous bargain in a Bexhill antique shop - 2 volumes of Paynes Dresden Gallery. According to Book Auction Records for 1987, they sold for £220; would I be interested in buying them for £130? And so I end up paying £130 in the afternoon, for books that I could have bought in the morning for £30. I take them to Dick to see if he wants to buy them from me.

"I'll just look them up in the latest Book Auction Records."

After a few moments delay, he informs me that by 1990 the price had slumped to £90, and he suggests that I really should have looked them up in my reference library before paying so much for them.

"I did," I inform him, but I do not elaborate.

Thursday 14th February

Oh, the joys of an English winter. The war in the Gulf goes on, southern England lies buried under a blanket of snow, and my back has seized up so badly that, whenever I attempt to move, I look like a grant applicant at the Ministry of Silly Walks.

I catch a train to Dulton in the certain knowledge that, even if the other dealers have seen the Hole and Pilchard sale advertised, they will find it almost impossible to drive there. British Rail are running about one train every three hours. According to a spokesman, their trains are not working because 'this is the wrong kind of snow.' Presumably if the snow was pink, warm, and falling upwards, it would cause no problems whatsoever.

When I eventually arrive at the saleroom, I am delighted to discover that only half a dozen other dealers have succeeded in making it through the snow. I am, though, disappointed to discover - but not surprised - that the Crawley ring are among that number.

The Crawley ring operate under the assumption that every book auctioned within their territory should, by rights, belong to them. Their tactics at auction are as follows -

1) Buy every lot as cheaply as possible, and then share them out afterwards amongst themselves.

2) Be prepared to bid all the way to a book's maximum value in order to stop anyone else making any money on it.

3) Stand up and laugh at anyone who outbids them by paying more for a book than it's worth. (It is not unusual for them to ridicule the buyer with such comments as: "I've got a copy of that book in my shop at half that price. Perhaps you'd like to buy that one as well.")

When the sale begins, I attempt to spend my £240 on several occasions, but each time I lose out to the ring. Most lots are bought unopposed by the ring for next to nothing.

I resist the temptation to launch into a violent assault on the ring's bollocks, and decide instead to put on my balaclava and leave. I am by the door when the auctioneer announces a lot that I somehow missed at the presale viewing.

"Malthus. Principles of Political Economy. Presentation copy. Annottated in the hand of Riccardo."

I am, of course, something of an authority on signed books. My ears prick up instinctively. (They don't move far because I've still got my balaclava on.) Occasionally I feel that fate is pushing me in a particular direction. This appears to be just such an occasion. I take off my balaclava and decide to buy the Malthus even if it means spending most of my £240 on it. I decide to buy the Malthus even if it means spending all of my £240 on it.

The bidding opens at £5,000, and I decide not to buy the Malthus after all. The Crawley ring drop out at £12,000, John from Brighton drops out at £19,000, and the book is bought by a young man called Finch for £45,000. I throw my catalogue in the bin, put on my balaclava, and head vaguely in the direction of Sevenoaks. Outside a large truck pulls up to take away the ring's purchases. I am too depressed even to kick it.

On the journey to Sevenoaks, I make up my mind that I have had my £240 for long enough. I move straight to the section marked 'EXTREMELY LARGE BOOKS', and search methodically through them for something suitable to spend it on.

When the sale begins, it is soon apparent that the preference amongst the other dealers is for smaller books, and I manage, without much opposition, to buy four enormous antiquarian books and a 19th century history of seashells.

At the back of my catalogue, I calculate how much money I have left to spend. At the back of my brain, I calculate how many more books I will have the strength to carry home. My calculations reveal that I still have plenty of money to spare, but very little strength. In the topography section, I manage to buy a two volume history of Bristol for £28, but it is now getting perilously close to the end of the sale and I still have £110 left to spend. The lot after the Bristol volumes is a 16th century history of Wales. I have not viewed the book, and I have no intention whatsoever of bidding for it. (I don't even know how big it is.) The bidding moves stutteringly to £100 and then stops. The nodding head that bids £110 is certainly mine, but it is not my conscious brain that instructs it to do so. No sooner have I made the bid, than I offer up a silent prayer that somebody in the room will outbid me. Nobody does.

And so my £240 is spent. I pile up my folio purchases, and I search optimistically among the larger books for my 16th century Welsh history. It is nowhere to be seen. Perhaps someone has stolen it and I'll be able to claim my money back. When it eventually turns up, it proves to be one of the smallest books I have ever seen. I can understand how an enormous book can be worth £110, but, surely, anyone paying £110 for a book as small as this must want their head examined. I grin at myself in the mirror.

My purchases fill two carrier bags and a rucksack. Despite my bad back, I discover that I just have sufficient strength to lift them off the floor; I do not, however, have sufficient strength to move myself from the position in which I am standing. Eventually, inch by inch, I manoeuvre myself down the stairs and onto the pavement. The auction room lies at the top of a steep hill; half a mile away at the bottom of an ice covered pavement is Sevenoaks Station. I balance myself precariously at the edge of the precipice and prepare to begin my descent.

Once I am in motion, there is no stopping me.

I find myself deposited on Platform 1, beneath a pile of large (and one small) antiquarian books, after a high speed journey which seems to be over after approximately 30 seconds. I arrive just in time to discover that the Hastings train has been cancelled, and that, in order to get home, I will have to change trains at Tonbridge.

I get off at Tonbridge and ask a porter which train I need to catch for St Leonards. He points behind me at the now moving train from which I have just disembarked. The carrier bags now feel as if they are filled with rocks. If it was a physical possibility, I'd hit him with them.

It is only when I arrive at St Leonards station that my luck appears to take a turn for the better; a taxi is waiting outside the ticket office. I shuffle forward as quickly as possible. About ten yards ahead of me, an antiquarian lady is hobbling through the snow, suitcase in one hand, walking stick in the other. She is moving unmistakably in the direction of the taxi rank. I put on a spurt and overtake her with about twenty yards to spare. About ten yards from the taxi, the lady reappears alongside me and we move towards the taxi, me shuffling, her hobbling, until we arrive together at the taxi door.

"Ladies first," exclaims the driver, as he takes the lady's bag with one hand and opens the door with the other.

"Bastards," I mutter under my breath.

St Leonards station is situated at the bottom of a steep hill; half a mile away at the top of the hill is my bookshop. I manage to progress approximately ten yards before I am forced to stop for a rest.

Once I have stopped, it is almost impossible to get started again.

In all, the final leg of my excursion takes well over an hour. It is the most tortuous journey I have experienced since I spent the entire night with my head stuck in the lavatory of an Indian railway carriage.

I fling my purchases on the bookshop floor and, with my last remaining ounce of energy, I pick up my copy of Book Auction Records. I am determined to find out if a 16th century book on Welsh history can possibly be worth the enormous amount of money I have paid for it. I open Book Auction Records and turn to the appropriate entry - 'CARADOC of Llancarfan, Historie of Cambria (1954) 7/6'.

I think this means that I have just made an expensive mistake. I am though, by now, too exhausted to be certain one way or the other. I am, by now, too exhausted to care.

Saturday 16th February

Cometh the moment, cometh the man, cometh the Nick Bernstein.

The first dealer to whom I show my Sevenoaks purchases is James. James genuinely loves antiquarian books. He loves them most of all when they belong to him. I know I can't have done too badly when he turns green with envy more quickly than the Six Million Dollar Man. (My mother-in-law tells me this should be the Incredible Hulk and she should know.)

We agree a price on two folio volumes, but when I mention how much I want for my Welsh history, he has to place his hand over his mouth in order to prevent himself from laughing out loud.

"I think I'll leave that one with you, Clive."

I pocket his £85, and begin to search in the 'Bookdealer' for specialists in Welsh books. There aren't any. With a sigh, I push the remainder of my purchases to one side and settle down to watch this afternoon's England v Scotland rugby match.

People often ask me why I became a bookseller.

"Because it gives me the freedom to be intellectually and spiritually independent," is my well rehearsed reply.

"Any other reasons?"

"Yes, it means I can watch lots of sport on television."

I switch on the television just as the game is about to start. No sooner have I done so, than a steady stream of customers begin to file into the shop. I know, from experience, that the more interesting the sport I am attempting to watch, the more customers I will have attempting to annoy me. If I'm watching something really tedious, like a 24 hour synchronised swimming marathon or a slow motion action replay of a Terry Griffiths snooker match, I probably won't see a soul all day. Come three o'clock on Cup Final Saturday, however, and I can guarantee there will be more breathing space on the Wembley terraces than there will be inside my shop.

It only needs a penalty to be awarded or a streaker to run across the pitch, and I can guarantee that Driffield will choose that exact moment to phone me up for one of his little chats (3 hours is a little chat for Driffield).

Unquestionably the most frustrating experience of all is watching the England cricket team batting. I only have to look away from the screen for a split second, and it is an absolute certainty that a couple of wickets will have fallen by the time I look back again. (I remember one occasion, when the entire team was bowled out in the time it took me to replace a book on the top shelf and return to my desk.)

During the course of this afternoon's rugby match, I manage to see the pre-match warm up, the half time studio discussion, a player running up to take a penalty kick, and the after match interviews. I turn off the television and make my final preparations for going home.

The last few minutes before five o'clock are undoubtedly the tensest of the working day. It is in this twilight zone that the 'ONE MINUTE TO FIVERS' operate. The 'ONE MINUTE TO FIVERS' are a secret society of shoppers, whose sole purpose in life is to enter shops as near to closing time as possible, in order to stop the proprietor from going home. They award each other points according to -

1) How near to closing time they manage to enter a
   shop.
2) How long they manage to stay in the shop before
   they are physically removed.

They are forbidden by the rules of the society from buying anything once they are inside the shop. My shop has always been a prime target for members of the society, because for years I never had the heart to throw anyone out. It was not unusual, in the old days, for me to still be here at nine o'clock at night waiting for the "ONE MINUTE TO FIVER" to make the next move.

Saturday is a particularly popular evening with "ONE MINUTE TO FIVERS" because, apparently, they score extra points for choosing the last day of the working week. At two minutes to five, I peer anxiously up and down an empty street. At one minute to five, a darkened figure emerges from the shadows and pushes against the door. My heart sinks. The figure that enters my shop is that of Nick Bernstein. My heart bobs back to the surface again.

Nick Bernstein is welcome at any time of the day. He buys

good books and he is prepared to pay well for them. He is clearly disappointed by the fact that there are more gaps on my shelves than there are books.

I take my remaining Sevenoaks purchases, and place them at discreet intervals around the shop. He shows no interest in a defective book by Sir Philip Sidney, but agrees, without hesitation, to buy the 2 volumes on Bristol, the history of seashells and an antiquarian book of theology. Only when he discovers the Welsh history is he clearly undecided. He fondles it in what seems an almost indecent manner before placing it back on the shelves.

"I'll phone you up about that one, Clive."

"You can have it ten pounds cheaper if you take it now."

"Done."

As Nick Bernstein leaves the shop, I reach out to shut the door behind him. Even as I attempt to do so, the blurred form of the president of the 'ONE MINUTE TO FIVERS' comes rushing past me into the shop. The president of the 'ONE MINUTE TO FIVERS' is more commonly known by his other title; 'Pain in the Arse'.

"Just a quick look round, if you don't mind. Not that I've got any money on me though."

I resist an overwhelming desire to tell him to piss off; sink back into my armchair and turn the television on.

The night is still young.

Wednesday 27th February

It is an amazing coincidence: every time I get on a train, I seem to end up sitting opposite a young girl wearing an incredibly short skirt. (The young girls are wearing the short skirts, not me.)

This morning's journey is no exception. After searching for about twenty minutes, I manage to find a girl in an incredibly short skirt and I sit down opposite her. It is not till I make eye contact with her at Wadhurst that I discover she is a Glen Close lookalike.

I have seen "Fatal Attraction" seventeen times, and my instinctive reaction is to find somewhere else to sit. All the other seats are occupied. She smiles at me hungrily. (At this moment the mobile buffet comes by. She buys three cheese rolls and a packet of chocolate biscuits. Blimey, she really is hungry.)

When she's finished eating, she smiles at me again. Not so hungrily this time. Chunks of cheese roll are clearly visible sticking to her teeth that glisten in the artificial light. She leans towards me.

"Going far?

"I'm a married man."

She places her hand firmly on my left kneecap.

"My favourite kind."

"With four children."

"Even better."

"And a bad back."

The pressure of her hand increases slightly.

"Did anybody ever tell you that you bear an almost uncanny resemblance to Michael Douglas?"

My first reaction is to agree with her wholeheartedly; my second reaction is to recognise that Jimmy Saville bears a closer resemblance to Michael Douglas than I do. (According to my mother, I am the splitting image of Prince Charles, but no one agrees with her, thank God.)

As the train makes progress up the railway line, Glen Close's hand makes progress up the inside of my trouser leg. We arrive at Charing Cross station in the nick of time. I decide to make a run for it. As soon as I am on the platform, I move as quickly as possible towards the ticket barrier; at least, the left hand side of my body moves quickly towards the ticket barrier. The right hand side of my body doesn't want to move at all. My back complaint is clearing up at a variable rate. The left hand side of my back is now fine, the right hand side is worse than ever. Glen Close approaches me on my right hand side.

"You promised me your name and phone number."

I scribble shakily on the sheet of paper that she thrusts towards me and continue my somewhat lopsided progress along the platform.

"I'll be in touch, Mr Driffield," she calls after me, but my left hand side is already out of earshot.

Outside the station I catch a bus to Chelsea. I now have £370 to spend: I got rid of the defective Philip Sidney by reducing its price by five pounds a day until James bought it for twenty pounds. (I once attempted to sell a set of Arthur Mees Childrens Encyclopedia by the same method, and ended up having to pay two legally minded small boys five pounds to take it away.)

I arrive at Bonhams auction room to discover that the books on offer are about as stimulating as an out of date copy of the Mail on Sunday. The only reasonable books they have are on far eastern travel; I phone Mr Crouch to see if he thinks they're worth my while buying. Mr Crouch is out buying books.

I resist the temptation to gamble my hard earned £370, and leave empty handed about half way through the sale. I spend the bus journey thinking up new mantras and studying the names above the Chelsea shopfronts. Halfway down the Kings Road, I discover a shop called R.SOLES. I make a note of it for future reference.

Later that evening, I telephone Mr Crouch and tell him about the far eastern books that were in the sale.

"If I'd managed to buy them for £370, how much would you have paid me for them?"

"About £700."

"R.SOLES."

"I beg your pardon."

"R.SOLES. It's the name of a shop in the Kings Road Chelsea. I had a feeling it's a name that would come in useful before too long."

Friday 1st March

A ceasefire has halted hostilities in the Gulf. Hostilities in the auction room continue unabated. Michael drives me to West Sussex, and we are forced to sit and watch as the Crawley ring buy every decent book that is offered in the first hour of the Paces auction. There is only so much a man can take.

I communicate to Michael, by means of sign language, that we should meet for a chat. "Where?" asks Michael in a mime which impresses me as both subtle and discreet. "In the men's toilet," I reply in a mime which is neither of these things.

The lady sitting opposite assumes I am some kind of pervert; the auctioneer assumes I am bidding, and I very nearly become the proud owner of a run of the 'Rose Annual'.

When Michael and I enter the lavatory at Paces auction, we do so as free spirited and independent bookdealers. The transformation we undergo in that lavatory is every bit as dramatic as that which Clark Kent undergoes in a telephone kiosk. When Michael and I emerge from the lavatory, we have become the Hastings ring.

There cannot be a person in the room who doesn't realise there is something significantly different about us. I prod Michael in the ribs.

"Your flies are undone," I inform him.

We each have our instructions. Michael will do the bidding; I will do the laughing at anyone who outbids us. The next two lots are knocked down to the Hastings ring, but when the Crawley ring purchases the lot that follows, Michael makes no effort whatsoever to enter into the bidding.

I laugh uproariously, inform the audience that they have just witnessed a world record auction price for a collection of Folio Society novels, and ask Michael what the hell happened to him.

"We've run out of money," he explains.

An hour, and much laughter later, we meet in the car park.

"What do rings do now?" asks Michael.

"They share out their books," I reply in a hoarse whisper.

The lots we have bought are a Heron edition collection of Joseph Conrad novels and a set of the Harmsworth Encyclopaedia.

Michael puts in the first claim.

"I definitely don't want the Conrad novels."

"Neither do I."

"And I've already got a set of Harmsworths."

"So have I."

After a lengthy dispute, my share turns out to be half a set of Conrad novels and the L-Z volumes of the Harmsworth Encyclopaedia.

"At least the Crawley ring didn't have it all their own way this time," I remark, but Michael isn't listening to me anymore.

Wednesday 6th March

At the bottom of a tea chest of books at the Julian Dawson weekly auction in Lewes, I make the discovery that changes everything -

'Malthus - The Principles of Political Economy' (signed copy, annottated by Riccardo). It is a coincidence that almost defies belief.

I look nervously around me, hide the book in the newspaper that lines the inside of the tea chest, and bury it beneath layer after layer of book club novels. The next hour is the most nerve racking of my life.

"Lot 100. A tea chest of books. Ten pounds to start me? Five if you will? A pound if you must."

I nod my head so violently, my balaclava drops down across my face.

"I have a bid of a pound. Anymore? Sold. Is that Mr Linklater?"

I pull back my balaclava to confirm my identity.

It is almost too easy to be true. I hand over my pound and begin to empty the tea chest. The books seem to go on forever. At the bottom I find a complete run of the Guinness book of records that I'm sure weren't there before. Beneath them in the newspaper I can feel the book that is going to make my fortune. I pull it open and study the title page. It reads -

'British Friesian Herd Book Vol 39.'

I rub my eyes in disbelief. Its frontispiece is a photograph of a cow. It stares at me and greets me in a highly unoriginal manner.

"Moo, moo."

There is something familiar about the cow's expression. It reaches uncowlike towards me and shakes me by the shoulders. The cow's face begins to blur and becomes my wife's face. The cow is my wife. My wife is a cow. (I mean that in the nicest possible way.)

"Moo, moove, moove, move yourself. It's three o'clock in the morning and its time to get up."

I open my eyes and look around me. There is no cow. Only my wife. It is three o'clock in the morning and it is time to get up.

A bookseller's life is not all glamour.

I am going to the Dominic Winter sale in Swindon, and there are two reasons why I want to begin my journey at this unearthly hour.

1) I am probably the slowest driver in the world. You know those drivers that pull out of side streets on Sunday afternoons and proceed to block your progress at speeds that fluctuate between 15 and 18 m.p.h. Well, I drive like them, only slower.

2) At three o'clock in the morning I can overtake lots of milk floats. (I can only overtake milk floats when they are moving very slowly indeed. Once they are moving at something approaching full speed, milk floats overtake me.)

I arrive at Swindon at ten o'clock, despite a nasty experience on the Winchester to Newbury dual carriageway, where I get caught in a following wind and completely lose control of my speed which rises to an alarming forty miles an hour. (There have been occasions in the past, when the wind has been coming in the opposite direction, that I have actually found myself travelling backwards.)

I am so exhausted by the time I get to Swindon, that all I want to do is turn around and go straight back home again. I decide to stay, only because most of the books in the section marked 'Antiquarian Continental Theology' are absolutely gigantic.

Prices on individual books are prohibitively high. There is certainly nothing on which it would be sensible to spend my £370. I buy two lots of antiquarian continental theology for stock and set out on my journey home.

At three o'clock in the morning, the impact of my speed on the traffic flow of others is minimal. At five o'clock in the afternoon, it can be catastrophic. By Petersfield, the queue behind me stretches all the way to the distant horizon. As I approach Billingshurst, there is a warning on Radio Sussex that a slow moving vehicle is causing a six mile tailback on the outskirts of town, and that drivers should avoid the area if at all possible. I am about to change direction when it occurs to me that the slow moving vehicle is mine. I notice that it is beginning to get dark; I turn on my lights and adjust my speed accordingly.

It is almost midnight when I get back to my shop. I decide it is not too late to telephone James and tell him about my purchases.

"Great news, James. I've managed to buy a collection of antiquarian continental theology."

"That's great news, Clive?"

I am concerned to hear that he ends the sentence with a question mark, rather than the half a dozen exclamation marks I had been expecting.

"They're antiquarian; that's good isn't it, James?"

"You mean they're old; yes, that's marvellous news."

"And they're continental; that's good isn't it, James?"

"You mean they're foreign; unfortunately that means that the few people who can understand them aren't the least bit interested in what they've got to say."

What I purchased was an impressive sounding collection of antiquarian continental theology. What I now have to try to sell has been transformed by James into a rather ordinary sounding load of old foreign religious books.

Swindon seems a long way to travel to buy a load of old foreign religious books that are pretending to be something that they're not.

A bloody long way.

26th March

£370 may be a lot of money; it is, though, proving insufficient to buy any of the decent books that are offered in the salerooms. I feel like a child who wants to buy a quarter of sweets, but only has enough money for two ounces. I purchase a county atlas for £50 in Hornsey, and spend the rest of the month watching the Crawley ring get richer.

Dick is clearly impressed when I show him the atlas.

"If you let me take it away, I'll come back in a minute and make you an offer on it you can't refuse."

He comes back two days later and offers me £50. I refuse it. I am beginning to have my doubts about Dick.

I continue to trust that all my hard work will eventually be rewarded. My planned timetable for this afternoon is typical.

1.15 p.m: Make my bi-weekly visit to Sam's Emporium.
3.00 p.m: Bid for lot 272 at Clifford Danns Lewes auction.
(Dick has commissioned me to pay £100 for part of an S.D.U.K. atlas.)
4.00 p.m: Attend the Sneering and Coleman sale in Poundbridge.

The notice outside Sam's reads -
'WARNING TO CUSTOMERS.
THE PROPRIETOR OF THIS ESTABLISHMENT
IS OBNOXIOUS, BELIGERENT, EXTREMELY
STUPID AND HARDLY EVER HERE'

It is a notice that could be appropriately displayed outside half the secondhand bookshops in the country. It is, though, most appropriate when applied to Sam.

Sam is in a particularly bad mood this afternoon, and he has two good reasons for being so -

1) His shop has been broken into by an unusually intelligent robber. The intruder ignored the books and made off with Sam's entire stock of pornographic videos. The police, under pressure since the release of the Birmingham six to arrest only suspects who might conceivably have committed the

crime, have no idea who did it. They tend to suspect someone who either sells or watches dirty movies.

2) Sam, in a moment of marital aberration, has sacked his wife. His wife is delighted. She hated working in the shop, was never paid a penny, and is now free to indulge in her passion for collecting old buttons. Sam is condemned to spend his days doing that which he hates most in life; serving customers.

On his shelves is a twenty seven volume collection of the 'Wayside and Woodland' natural history series. It is priced at £250.

"Any chance of doing these any cheaper, Sam?"

"What are you offering?"

"150?"

"Go on then," he concedes wearily.

There is a danger for any bookseller who bargains so openly within the hearing of their other customers. Every other person in the room will expect their books at a reduced price. The elderly lady standing behind me in the queue attempts to take advantage of Sam's apparent good mood. She pushes a Mills and Boon paperback in Sam's direction.

"Could you do this one any cheaper then?"

Sam snatches the book from her grasp, opens it roughly, and rips it in half. The book, I notice, is called 'Tender Moments'.

"Half price to you love," declares Sam, as he thrusts the two halves back into the hands of a decidedly bewildered customer.

I check my watch; two o'clock and I am well behind schedule. I have approximately an hour to drive the twenty five miles to Lewes. Impossible you might say. I abandon the habits of a lifetime and begin to drive like a maniac. By the time I reach the marsh road I am cruising at a steady twenty eight miles an hour.

I stop to pick up two female hitchhikers, but they decline my offer on the grounds that they're trying to get somewhere in a bit of a hurry. I notice them, ten minutes later, waving to me from the back of a tractor that overtakes me on the Pevensey bypass. At a quarter to three, I am still five miles from the saleroom. My progress through the hills that surround Lewes is like a slow motion action replay of the "Bullit" car chase. I park in the High

Street and leap through the door of Clifford Danns auction room. As I do so, I say a silent prayer: "Please, please, please God, let me be in time for lot 272."

"Lot 274," comes the voice of a Lewes auctioneer.

"Shit," comes the voice of a Hastings bookseller.

I ask the man standing next to me if he knows how much lot 272 sold for. "£420," he informs me. If, at this moment, I was asked to compile a list of those booksellers whose knowledge and expertise I most admire, Dick's name would most assuredly not be among them. I buy myself a packet of chocolate drops, to console myself, and begin the journey to Poundbridge. I might as well have gone straight home.

The Sneering and Coleman sale takes on a now familiar pattern. The books I am interested in are a copy of the Munich Gallery and a plate book on the Bosphorus. Unfortunately for me, the Crawley ring are interested in the same books. The auctioneer smiles at me sympathetically and continues on his word perfect way.

Auctioneering is a profession which demands a great degree of verbal dexterity. Today's auctioneer progresses smoothly until three lots from the end of the sale, without putting a single word out of place. His first slip of the tongue, when it does come, arrives at a particularly unfortunate moment.

Hillaire Belloc is an author whose works do not command a great deal of attention within the secondhand booktrade. Normally, a lot described in an auction catalogue as "a collection of old Bellocs" would pass with little interest and even less bidding. When the auctioneer announces it as a "load of old Bollocs", it causes uproar. It is an error that clearly appeals to the somewhat basic humour of the assembled audience.

When I drive home this evening, there is no Munich Gallery in the boot of my car; there is no plate book on the Bosphorus. There are no Bollocs.

Thursday 4th April

Spring; season of the mini-skirt, the boot sale, and the poll tax demand.

I drive my eleven year old son to the first major bootsale of the year at Maidstone. The sum total of my purchases for myself is a book entitled 'The Pleasures of Parenthood'. The sum total of my purchases for my eleven year old son is an Arsenal video, a hamburger with onions, a can of coca cola, and a stick of candyfloss. Driving back through Tonbridge, my eleven year old son is sick all over my book entitled 'The Pleasures of Parenthood'. In the next six months, I will, in all probability, visit something like a hundred boot sales. They can only get better.

The auctions, if anything, are getting steadily worse. I visit Broad Heath book auction, but however many times I nod my head to bid, a prominent member of the Crawley ring raises his eyebrows to outbid me. One day he'll raise his eyebrows once too often and he'll find they won't come down again. (It is an accepted fact that, just as dog owners come to resemble their pets, so bookdealers come to resemble their bidding styles. You can always tell a retired bookseller by the fact that there is invariably at least one facial function over which he has no semblance of control whatsoever.)

Only when I bid sixty pounds for a Charles Traylen reprint of London views, do I have any success. My pleasure is tempered, somewhat, by the unusually prolonged outburst of hilarity that greets my purchase. At least two members of the Crawley ring have to leave the room, they're laughing so much.

I am extremely relieved when, within ten minutes of returning to my shop, I sell the book to a London print dealer for a hundred pounds. Dick is clearly impressed when I tell him about it.

"You did do well."

"Why's that then?"

"It's still available new for twenty five pounds."

I now have to spend the next ten years hoping that a reputedly violent London print dealer doesn't discover this fact for himself.

It occurs to me that the only satisfying purchase I have made recently is the collection of 'Wayside and Woodland' books that I bought from Sam. I know he has a ballet book signed by Sitwell (I am an authority on signed books) that he's trying to sell for a hundred pounds. It occurs to me that if he were prepared to sell me another £120 of books (this is beginning to get complicated), I would be able to spend all £370 with Sam.

I decide to go to Sam and throw myself on his mercy.

"Oi, get off my mercy, you're squashing it."

"Sorry Sam. I've come to ask you for your assistance."

"I've sacked them all."

"If I buy your ballet book for a hundred pounds, would you sell me another £120 worth of books?"

"I'll bring them round tonight."

At nine o'clock, the Sammobile pulls up outside my house. A shadowy figure emerges from the darkness and approaches my front door. It is Sam and he is carrying a box of books. I hand over my remaining £220.

My £370 is thus invested in: 27 volumes of the 'Wayside and Woodland' series, 1 ballet book (signed by Sitwell), and a miscellaneous collection of books ranging from Enid Blyton first editions to an illustrated copy of the Karma Sutra.

Normally, such a collection would blend into my stock and take at least until next Christmas to shift. There is a Bloomsbury sale on Thursday that I'm keen to attend: I give myself until then at the latest to sell the lot of them.

Friday 12th April

I must be getting old. I buy a book from Michael entitled 'The Memoirs of an Erotic Bookseller', and I find myself skipping over the dirty bits in order to get to the bits about bookselling.

By Thursday, all the books that I bought from Sam are sold. There is good news and there is bad news. The good news is that I sell the 'Wayside and Woodland' volumes for £250. The bad news is that my profit on the remaining books (for which I paid £220) is a measly £5. It works out at a profit margin of 2%.

I sell the children's books easily enough: to two middle aged women. Anyone who imagines you can sell children's books to children would be sadly mistaken. Today's children are not interested in books entitled 'Noddy and Big Ears spend a day at the Seaside' or 'Dimsie wins through'. To sell a book to a child nowadays, you need to put the book in a cover showing a selection of severed limbs or a face with green slime pouring out of its nostrils. If middle aged women didn't buy children's books, then nobody would.

I sell the ballet book for what I paid for it, and practically give the remaining books away to Robert on Wednesday evening. At least all the books are sold, and I now have £475 to take to Bloomsbury on Thursday morning. I never get there.

I am driving to the station when a poster in a shop window attracts my attention.

'MAMMOTH BOOK SALE.

CHURCH HALL. FRIARS WALK. LEWES.'

My immediate reaction is to be put off by the word mammoth. In my experience, the bigger it is claimed a sale will be, the smaller it will prove to be in reality. I once went to a bootsale advertised as *'POSITIVELY THE MOST GIGANTIC BOOTSALE IN THE ENTIRE HISTORY OF BOOTSALES'*, only to discover, when I arrived, that it consisted of one man selling absolute rubbish from the back of his moped. On the other hand, I have been to bootsales advertised as *'EXTREMELY MODESTLY SIZED BOOTSALES'* and discovered, when I arrived, that the row of stalls stretched all the way to the distant horizon.

My second reaction to the poster is to change direction and

head for Lewes. I have never been any good at resisting booksales held in Church halls. My third reaction is to change direction again and head back towards the station. I have never been any good at taking decisions.

Decisions worry me. It disturbs me to think that every decision you take has the potential to change your life. Turn left when you leave home in the morning and you might just find a twenty pound note lying in the gutter. Turn right and you might still find a twenty pound note in the gutter, but just at the moment when you bend down to pick it up, a bus might come along and squash you flat. My problem is that, however much thought I give to a decision, I invariably end up making the wrong choice.

If I choose Lewes, it is an absolute certainty that I could have spent my £475 at Bloomsbury. If I choose Bloomsbury, there is no doubt whatsoever that news will reach me of the unbelievable bargains that I missed at Lewes. I finally settle on Bloomsbury, and then change my mind and head for Lewes instead.

I calculate that, if I go to Lewes and leave after half an hour, there will just be enough time for me to get to Bloomsbury. I do believe it is one of the most impressive decisions I have ever made.

I am the first to arrive outside the Lewes booksale. I anxiously watch the approaching pathway to see who will be joining me in the queue. Out of the first ten people to join me, eight are bookdealers. So far, though, so good. No Brownies. When the booksale opens, the queue stretches for about two hundred yards and contains virtually every bookdealer in Sussex. There is not a Brownie to be seen. Perhaps I have made the right decision after all.

The sale begins at 10.00a.m. Thursday. To get to Bloomsbury on time, it is essential that I leave by 10.30. I leave at 10.30 exactly: 10.30 Friday. It is a mammoth booksale in every sense of the word. There are vast quantities of books and it goes on for three consecutive days.

Every time I find a book to buy, an assistant rushes up and fills the gap on the shelves with an equally enticing volume. It's like the tale of 'The Magic Porridge Pot'; the books just keep coming and coming. I fill up the boot of my car on Thursday, and return on Friday to see what new stock has been put out overnight. Not once do I think of Bloomsbury. Not once do I doubt that I made the correct decision.

When I unload the books at my shop, I find I have acquired sufficient stock to keep me solvent for the next month. All I need to do now is find a place where I can spend my £475. I could go to the Maidstone antiques fair on Saturday. I could wait till Tuesday for the Ardingly Spring Fair. I could do both.

Decisions, decisions.

Tuesday 16th April

I really am getting old. I see from my dream diary that I have not had an erotic dream for the last six weeks. All I seem to dream about now is books. The night before the Maidstone antiques fair, it would have been more appropriate if my dreams had been about bacon rolls. That's all I manage to buy.

I decide that, if I'm going to Ardingly, it is vital that I get in early. I discover that there are two accepted methods for achieving this.

1) THE PAY A VAST AMOUNT OF MONEY METHOD.

Antique fairs are the only events I know that make a Frank Sinatra concert look like good value for money. (Come to think of it, they have a lot in common: both involve you paying a lot of money to look at something that is old and over-rated.) A ticket for pre-sale viewing at Ardingly costs £35.

2) THE TROJAN HORSE METHOD.

This is a method (alternatively known as the very large wardrobe method) that is organised by local antique dealer, Reg Marley. The method is simple; a large wardrobe is placed inside the back of Reg Marley's van and a large number of antique dealers are placed inside the wardrobe. Reg then pays his £35 and drives the antique dealers (still inside the wardrobe) into Ardingly antiques fair. By this method, approximately twenty dealers manage to get in for the price of one.

I mention to Reg that I am hoping to get in early to this week's fair.

"Any room for one more in the wardrobe?" I enquire.

"I'm sure we can squeeze you in," he replies.

That night, for the first night in weeks, I do not dream about books. I dream about being confined in a wardrobe with a large number of antique dealers. In the morning, I tell Reg Marley I have changed my mind. £35 suddenly doesn't seem such a lot of money after all.

I drive to Ardingly and hand over my money. It hurts. For the next four hours I drag myself around approximately a thousand antique stalls. I do not buy a single book. I had always assumed that antique stalls were filled with overpriced crap because all the bargains had been sold before I got there. Now I realise they are filled with overpriced crap because overpriced crap is all they had to start with.

I come to the conclusion that the £35 it cost me to get in is, without doubt, the worst investment I have made in my life.

I am about to leave when I discover, on a stall by the exit, a book on salmon fishing worth approximately thirty pounds. A small girl, about eight years old, has been left in charge of the stall. I sense a 'window of opportunity'.

"How much for this book?"

"Fifty."

"Fifty what?"

"Just fifty."

It is apparent that she is understandably perplexed by the intricacies of 'antique speak'.

"Fifty pence?"

"I suppose so."

For all I know the book may indeed be priced at fifty pence. I do not stop to find out. I hand over my money and move away as quickly as possible. When I glance over my shoulder, I am being pointed out by the girl to a large father like figure. He begins to run after me.

I hide behind the nearest available piece of furniture. It happens to be a large wardrobe. My pursuer goes hurtling past and I am about to move on, when I notice that an awful groaning sound is coming from the inside of the wardrobe.

It is a groaning that appears to comprise of several different voices. If there is a message in the groaning it would appear to be -

"For God's sake, get us out of here."

I point out the noise to the stallholder, who happens to be Reg Marley. He confirms that it has not gone unnoticed.

"Terrible isn't it. It's been going on all day. We forgot to bring the key with us."

I leave the Ardingly antiques fair, convinced that the £35 it cost me to get in is the best investment I have made in my life.

Thursday 18th April

I have never been over fond of people who order their Chinese takeaways by telephone. It has always irritated me that, while I have to wait for an hour to be served, other people can pull up in their cars, hand over their money, and be on their way home with their chop sueys and fried balls in less than a minute. (I wouldn't want to hang around if I had fried balls.)

I have always refused to order in this way. My reasons are as follows -

1) I believe it is morally unacceptable to do so. In my view, all men are created equal and should expect to be treated as such. It is wrong that one man should receive preferential treatment over another.
2) I have never had a telephone.

Equally, I have never been over fond of people who buy at auction without actually attending the sale. At today's Phillips London sale, the majority of lots are sold to buyers who have bid by either letter or telephone.

It is a method of doing business that clearly meets with the approval of the auctioneer. Each time a lot is sold this way, he positively sings out the words 'Commission Bidder'.

Each time he does so, he seems to be looking at the people in the room and saying, "Well, you're a lot of wankers aren't you. You travel all the way to London, you sit through this incredibly boring sale, and you still allow yourself to be outbid by someone who's sitting at home in the comfort of their living room".

Mostly he appears to be looking at me.

I ask the man sitting next to me why the commission bidders are more successful than we are.

"They're richer than us."

"But why?"

"Because they don't waste their time spending all day at auctions where they can't afford to buy a thing."

It is obvious that I have chosen to sit next to a particularly cynical member of the book trade.

I decide to alter my plans and, rather than rushing back to the local Hastings auction rooms, I telephone them from a call box instead.

"I'd like to leave a commission bid on Lot 340, the run of leather bindings"

It is a method of bidding that brings an almost instant reward. I learn that evening, from Michael, that the bindings were bought by the Crawley ring, who unexpectedly turned up at the sale. My reward is the fact that I didn't have to be there to watch them doing it.

Ordering by telephone has, after all, got a lot to be said for it.

Monday 29th April

You can tell it's spring by the fact that lambs and cricketers are frolicking in the fields. You can tell it's an English spring by the fact that there are snowflakes settling on the heads of the lambs and the cricketers as they frolic.

The latest notice in Sam's Emporium reads:

'HE WHO TALKS MOST
HAS THE LEAST TO SAY.
KINDLY SHUT UP'

You could hear a bookworm break wind; the customers are so quiet.

Sam's having less and less success at keeping customers out. However many barriers he puts in their way, they seem to succeed in clambering over them. His latest tactic is to allow the customers into the shop, and then to throw them out en masse once they're in there.

"I'm shutting now, so everyone clear out," is a cry Sam makes at intervals that bear no relation to the opening hours displayed on the shop door. Even customers queueing to pay for their purchases are herded out of the shop empty handed.

Sam is almost unique among booksellers in that he actually prefers dealers to members of the public. *'DEALERS ONLY'* is a notice that is regularly displayed outside the emporium.

Today is one of those days when Sam has clearly had enough of the general public.

"Dealers only from now on: everyone else get out," he announces without prior warning. The effect of this ultimatum is to make every normal looking person in the shop move towards the exit. The only people who remain are exactly the ones you'd be reluctant to allow into your shop in the first place.

I notice that a selection of railway books has appeared on the shelves since my last visit.

"Nice railway books, Sam. Any more where they came from?"

"Nine box loads."

Subconsciously, I calculate how many railway books it takes to fill nine boxes. Subconsciously, I calculate whether such a quantity would be worth offering £475 for. I test the water.

"If I offered £475 for them, would you accept it?"

"Too bloody right I would."

The water is hot to the touch.

When Sam brings the boxes from his storeroom, they are smaller than I'd imagined. The books that fill them less enticing than I'd hoped. I am about to turn them down when Sam makes a suggestion.

"Take them with you and have the afternoon to think about it."

One by one I lift up the boxes. My back groans. One by one I pile the boxes into the back of my car. My car groans. It is the heaviest load I have had to move since I gave my mother-in-law and her friend a lift to Weight Watchers.

When I price the books up, they add up to £513. It isn't a deal that, by any stretch of the imagination, makes financial sense. I telephone Old Gallery Bookshop, Hythe, (to whom I sold my last collection of railway books). I can get no reply.

I am about to return the books to my car, when Wilf Smith (to whom I had originally intended to sell my last collection of railway books) walks into the shop. He buys this latest collection for £525.

In the evening, I pay Sam my £475. If anyone is doing well out of my experiment it is Sam. Driving home, I ask myself if this particular deal was really worth my while.

The rustling of banknotes in my wallet suggests that it probably was. The horrible creaking noises, that are coming either from my back or the underneath of my car, suggest that it almost certainly wasn't.

Wednesday 1st May

It is my considered opinion that summer doesn't really begin until Sussex are knocked out of the Benson and Hedges Cup. I never have to wait too long. By my definition, summer has already begun.

The weather is typical summer weather. Antarctic summer weather. I drive to the Sandwich boot sale and make two purchases.

1) A pair of gloves to prevent frostbite

2) A sandwich.

At my stage of life, it gives me poetic satisfaction to be eating a sandwich in Sandwich. (In my younger days, my poetic satisfaction was obtained by a fortnight's holiday in Phuket, Thailand.) As sandwiches go, it is a very good sandwich; but then you'd expect that of a Sandwich sandwich.

The auctions are like the local buses; you wait ages for one to arrive and then loads of them turn up together. None of them seem able to take me in the direction I wish to travel.

I take my £525 to Godalming and fail to spend it. My problems are compounded by the fact that I am being consistently outbid by a child prodigy who has appeared unexpectedly on the auction scene. It is annoying to be outbid at any time; it is especially annoying when it's done by a twelve year old in school uniform.

Like most child prodigies, he looks about forty five years old, and will probably look younger than he does now in twenty years time. He either has extremely wealthy parents, or an unbelievably well paid paper round. He will, without doubt, be a millionaire by the time he's fifteen. It's at times like this when you ask yourself where it's all gone wrong.

Halfway through the sale, the prodigy grabs his satchel and rushes out. In the distance, I can hear a school bell faintly ringing. I redouble my concentration.

I have already accepted it is not a sale at which I can further my experiment. My priority now is to buy more than Michael. Michael could not, by any stretch of the imagination, be described as a child prodigy. He is, though, at auction, a rival.

There is nothing more frustrating than failing to buy a single book at an auction, and then having to watch as the other Hastings dealers carry off their purchases. So far, though, Michael, like me, has failed to buy a book.

About ten minutes before the end of the sale, I successfully bid £85 for a quantity of topographical books. I catch Michael's eye (er, disgusting) and stick my thumb in the air in triumph. Michael's complexion turns the colour of someone about to be violently sick.

About five minutes before the end of the sale, Michael bids successfully for a collection of art books. I sense that Michael is almost certainly looking in my direction (presumably with the eye I didn't catch); I look fixedly the other way.

After the sale, we queue up together to pay for our purchases.

"I see we both bought about the same amount today," comments Michael.

Oh well, one point for a draw is better than nothing.

When my turn comes to be served, the box containing my topographical books turns out to be so big that it takes two muscle-bound porters to lift it. I stand unsteadily beneath it and wait for Michael.

Michael's box of art books is carried towards him by a frail old lady who's about ninety five years old. She's holding it outstretched in the palm of her hand. It would more accurately be described as an extremely small carton, and in a previous existence it was probably used to display half a dozen Mars bars on a sweet shop counter.

To get to our cars, we have to carry our purchases down a flight of steep wooden steps. I am about to begin my descent beneath my enormous burden, when I turn towards Michael.

"Need any help with those, mate?" I enquire.

Three points for a win to me, I do believe.

Thursday 9th May

My philosophy of life is that if you can't make up your mind between two choices, you don't really want to do either of them. Today, I can't decide between Michael Shortalls Tunbridge Wells auction or the latest Bloomsbury sale.

At 8.34am, I disregard my philosophy of life, get on the Charing Cross train with Michael, and head for Bloomsbury. It is all I can do to stop myself getting off at Tunbridge Wells.

A quick inspection of the books at Bloomsbury tells me I have made a mistake. There is hardly a book that interests me. I calculate that it is still theoretically possible for me to get to Michael Shortalls for the start of the sale. Saying nothing to Michael (who has gone for a drink), I leave the auction room and begin to run.

I will need to run non-stop to the tube station; I will need an underground train to come almost immediately; I will need luck with my connection at Charing Cross; I will need a taxi to be waiting at Tunbridge Wells. I will need to have taken my train ticket with me.

I have been running for nearly twenty minutes, when I remember that I have left my train ticket (inside my bag) on a chair at Bloomsbury. It would take a fit man to recover from such a setback. I am not a fit man. (I actually gave up jogging when I found I was being overtaken by dogs that were walking past me.) I abandon my journey to Tunbridge Wells and walk dejectedly back to Hardwick Street.

My pessimism is proved to be justified. The few lots in which I am vaguely interested sell for more than I can afford to pay. My only consolation is that Michael's having no luck either. I resign myself to returning home empty-handed and drift into a gentle slumber.

I am rudely awoken by the sound of the auctioneer announcing Michael's name. My opening eyes are greeted by the sight of Michael grinning broadly.

"Any chance of some help with my books, mate?" enquires my rival.

Three points to him, I do believe.

It is only when I notice Michael in agitated conversation with the auctioneer, that I begin to suspect that something is amiss.

On the journey home, Michael refuses to let me see his purchases. For someone who has achieved such a notable victory, he seems unusually subdued.

"Something the matter?"

"Nothing."

I am not convinced by his denial. Teardrops, I notice, are forming in his eyes as he gazes out of the train window.

"You can tell me. It might help."

A single teardrop begins to move gently down across his cheek.

"I bought the wrong lot."

Once the teardrops have begun to flow, there is no stopping them. It is a pitiful sight to watch a grown man break down before my eyes. Between bouts of violent sobbing, he informs me that when he went to collect Lot 332, he was handed Lot 331. He had made the elementary mistake of losing concentration towards the end of a boring sale.

I decide that this is not the time for gloating. (That can come later.)

"Perhaps the books you bought aren't too bad anyway."

"I can't bear to look."

"Let me."

The first book I pull from the carrier bag is by John Morley. It is a bad start. Books by John Morley are 'dogs'. Books by John Morley are, indeed, the 'Great Danes' of secondhand bookselling. Compared to books by John Morley, copies of the British Friesian Herd Book sell like hot cakes. There cannot be a bookshop in the country that doesn't have a selection of John Morley volumes as a permanent part of stock.

I attempt to think of something to say that would cheer Michael up. Nothing comes readily to mind.

I reach into the bag and pull out the second book. It is by John Morley. It is bound in an identical fashion to the first volume. The third and fourth books that emerge confirm my worst suspicions. They are, there is no disguising the fact, by John Morley. The lot that Michael has mistakenly purchased comprises of a fifteen volume set of the works of John Morley.

As the 'Great Danes' of secondhand bookselling go, Michael has purchased the Crufts champion.

I lay the books across my lap. Words fail me.

Once I start laughing, there is no stopping me. Even Michael, the tears still flowing, joins in.

The three points, I do believe, are mine after all.

The championship, I do believe, is won.

Monday 13th May

I am becoming increasingly concerned about the direction in which my experiment is taking me. It now seems that -

1) Each time I spend my money, I am buying a larger quantity of books than I did the time before.
2) Each time I sell the books, my profit margin is lower than it was the time before.

I draw a graph to ascertain exactly what the consequences of these trends might be. It indicates that, by October, my final purchases will require a pantechnicon to move them. It indicates that my profit on them will be approximately £3.50.

Drastic action is called for. Plan B is called for.

The first requirement of Plan B is that I have to leave my wife and family.

At five o'clock in the morning, I creep out of bed and begin to write. It proves to be the hardest letter I have ever had to write. (After ten minutes, dawn breaks, and I find that I have forgotten to take the top off the pen. It isn't such a hard letter to write once the pen top is removed.) The letter reads -

"Dear Lesley and children,

I have left home. I hope you can forgive me. There are times in a man's life when a man has to take decisions that hurt the people he loves most.

See you Friday.
Love Clive"

Plan B has been fermenting in my brain for a number of weeks now. In a way, I suppose, Plan B has been fermenting in my brain throughout my life: there is, after all, something of the explorer in all of us.

Plan B reads -

DRIVE ROUND THE BOOKSHOPS, ANTIQUE SHOPS AND JUNK SHOPS OF ENGLAND UNTIL MY £525 IS SPENT.

I will not return until every last penny is spent (or Friday, whichever comes first). In my bag, I have a toothbrush and a guide book to antique shops that Michael has lent me. (The set of John Morley was in his window priced at exactly what he paid for them. He should be so lucky.)

I go round the house and, one by one, kiss my sleeping children gently on their foreheads. In my wife's bed, the face that I have loved for so many years is visible just above the bedspread; the pert nose, the dimpled cheeks. A thrill of appreciation runs through my body. I kiss the forehead gently.

Next to my teddy bear, my wife lies snoring loudly. I do not kiss her in case I wake her up.

The image of my children sleeping peacefully is the one that I will carry with me throughout the week. I shut the front door quietly and kick over half a dozen empty milk bottles. Behind me, I can hear the sound of a houseful of children waking up. I get in my car and head west.

Plan B does not promise a decrease in the quantity of books on which I will spend my money; it does, though, offer the potential of a decent return on my investment. Two weeks ago, I bought a leather bound set of Winston Churchill in an Eastbourne junk shop for £18: it was worth £150. It has convinced me that there are treasures to be found in the junk shops of England.

There aren't any treasures in the junk shops of Haywards Heath; there aren't any treasures in the junk shops of Petworth; I don't find a single treasure in any of the junk shops in any of the towns between Hastings and Southsea. I enter Portsmouth with an empty boot and an empty stomach. I am beginning to develop an intense aversion towards Plan B.

My philosophy of life is that however bad things seem, there are always others in the world with far worse problems than me. Take, for example, the driver stuck in front of me in the Portsmouth traffic. The smoke pouring from the rear end of his car would seem to indicate that he has a very serious problem indeed. When he drives forward, the smoke does not go with him; it hovers over the bonnet of my car. I check the temperature gauge; it is just entering the zone which reads - *PULL OVER QUICKLY. YOUR CAR IS ABOUT TO EXPLODE.*

I have driven a hundred miles, I have failed to buy a book, and my car has broken down. I spend the two hours that I have to wait for the AA man considering alternatives to Plan B.

The look that the AA man gives me is not a promising one. If your doctor looked at you like that, you'd know you didn't have long to live.

"You won't be going far in this."

I ask for a second opinion. The second opinion is given by a garage mechanic wearing a black cap. It is worse than the first opinion. He charges me £74 and advises me to head home. My car is only worth £30.

As I leave Portsmouth, I head east. I drive to Michael's and hand him back his guide to antique shops. The set of John Morley in his window suddenly doesn't seem as funny as it did before.

My children are preparing a sign that was intended to read -
WELCOME HOME DAD

At the moment I walk in the front door, it reads -
W

It's good to be home.

Sunday 19th May

My experiment has progressed to Plan C, which reads -
*DRIVE ROUND THE BOOKSHOPS, ANTIQUE SHOPS, JUNK
SHOPS AND BOOT SALES OF ENGLAND (PROVIDED THEY
ARE WITHIN A 35 MILE RADIUS OF HASTINGS) UNTIL MY
£525 IS SPENT.*
My first visit is to Sam's, where the notice on the door reads -
SOLD OUT OF:
BACON
BICYCLES
BUDGERIGARS
BUSES
BLOOMERS
B.P. 4-STAR

BOOKS ONLY INSIDE

Sam's been so busy writing notices, he hasn't had time to buy
any new stock. His only recent acquisition is a collection of
Readers Digest condensed novels. They are priced at 25p each.
They are a perfect illustration of Law 4 of bookselling. It reads -
*THE PRICE CHARGED FOR READERS DIGEST CONDENSED
NOVELS RISES IN AN INVERSE RELATIONSHIP TO THE
QUALITY OF THE BOOKSHOP SELLING THEM.*
My mother-in-law is constantly demanding to be taught more
about bookselling. I tell her about Law 4.
"You what?" she comments.
I get the feeling that Law 4 is a bit advanced for someone
still struggling to come to terms with the price structure of
secondhand Mills and Boon paperbacks.
Put simply, Law 4 means that the more downmarket the
bookshop, the more they will charge for their Readers Digest
condensed novels. A posh bookshop would put condensed novels
in their 'free' box. A charity shop would charge about two pounds
each for them.
The books in charity shops are the most expensive in the
world. The reason for this is that the women who work in charity

shops are the most miserable women in the world. They couldn't bear the sight of someone getting a bargain. (There is actually a fundraising scheme in the third world that raises money to send to the women who work in charity shops, in the hope that this might cheer them up.)

I leave Sam's empty handed, in the direction of the bootsales, and Law 5 of secondhand bookselling. Law 5 reads -

THE LATER YOU GO TO A BOOTSALE, THE MORE LIKELY YOU ARE TO FIND SOMETHING WORTH BUYING.

It is a myth that it is necessary to arrive at a bootsale at the crack of dawn. Go to a bootsale at seven o'clock in the morning, and every time you dive into a box of books, you will find that half a dozen other bookdealers have leapt in with you. Stroll into a bootsale at lunchtime, and the stallholders will be begging you to take their remaining stock off their hands.

I enter the bootsale in Eastbourne just as Michael is preparing to leave it. If ever I have needed Law 5 of bookselling to be proved correct, it is here and now.

The book that confirms it is indeed correct is a 19th century music manuscript that I buy for £15. (Michael tells me later that he had been offered the same book for £50.) I have no idea what it's worth, but I am excited enough by it to want to carry it around with me for the rest of the day.

The manuscript consists of the handwritten score to a Rossini opera. It is, in all probability, simply a finely produced copy. There is, though, a remote chance that it is something infinitely more exciting. The longer I hold it, the more excited I become. I tell my wife.

"I've got a feeling we're about to make our fortune."

She asks for a closer look, while I lean back and plan for the next thirty years of leisure.

"Good news, love!" my wife exclaims.

"How's that?"

"There's an original Beethoven in here as well!"

I lean back and plan for the next thirty years of bootsales.

Wednesday 22nd May

There is a poetic side to my nature.

The poetic side of my nature tells me it would be appropriate if the capital now accumulated by my experiment began to decline, and I ended the year with a book worth £2.50. I mention the idea to Michael.

"Couldn't agree with you more, Clive. Perhaps you'd like to start by giving me £525 for my set of John Morley."

If I followed Michael's advice, I could get from £525 to £2.50 in one simple transaction. There is, however, a mercenary side to my nature.

The mercenary side of my nature tells me I should be trying to make as much money from my experiment as possible. Where poetry and money do battle, there can, inevitably, be only one winner.

I abandon Plan C in favour of Plan D. It reads -

WORK WITHOUT A PLAN

The first opportunity that it provides for spending more of my £525 is at the Battle auction. A dealer who shall be nameless (Mr Crouch) commissions me to pay £150 for two Chinese books that are in the sale. Before doing so, he insists that I describe their condition to him in the greatest possible detail. I do so as follows -

"They're falling to bits; their covers are missing; they're badly stained; they give every sign of having been attacked by a small army of extremely hungry rodents; and that's just their good points."

I buy them for £100, and the dealer who shall be nameless (Mr Crouch) declines to buy them on the grounds that their condition is worse than he'd been led to expect. I place them beneath my desk on top of the Rossini score, put what's left of my money in my wallet, and head for Sam's.

Sam is missing. Attached to his door is a note which reads-

GONE TO BUY A ROLL OF BARBED WIRE FENCING

Presumably the time to start worrying is when he turns up for work one morning armed with a sub-machine gun.

I drive home, pick up my wife and baby daughter, and head for the John Bellman auction in Wisborough Green. My wife has decided that I am in need of some company on my travels. All the way to Battle, my wife provides me with some positively sparkling company. At Battle, she falls asleep. Between Battle and Wisborough Green, my only company is provided by my 18 month old daughter.

Having started our family with three boys, my wife and I have watched the development of our daughter with enormous interest. Her first word was awaited with great anticipation. Her first word, when it came, was 'football'. It is, up to the present moment, the only word she has managed.

Just outside Battle, I ask my daughter if there's any subject she'd particularly like to talk about.

"Football," she informs me, grinning broadly.

"Anything else?"

"Football," she repeats, and looks expectantly in my direction.

It's a long way from Battle to Wisborough Green. By the time we arrive at our destination, I don't believe there's an aspect of football that we haven't discussed exhaustively. We debate the sanity of a society where football managers can earn more in a fortnight than schoolteachers are paid in a year. We debate the possibility that the new England football manager will one morning be found drowned in a pool of his own verbal diarrhoea. And each time I pause for breath, my daughter enters the conversation with the same single worded contribution.

"Football," she comments, and waits for me to continue talking. We may not have the repartee of Saint and Greavsie, but at least I'm getting more response from my daughter than I am from my wife, who continues to lie slumped across the back seat, snoring loudly.

At Wisborough Green, my wife wakes up just long enough to make the observation,

"I don't think going to auction is as tiring as you make out, Clive," and promptly falls asleep again.

In the course of the John Bellman auction, I dispose of a percentage of my £525 on a set of early flying annuals and some bound volumes of the Illustrated London News.

When we start out on the journey home, my wife continues to

sleep soundly in the back seat.

"And what shall we talk about now?" I enquire of my daughter, as if I didn't already know the answer.

"Football," she suggests.

And so we do, all the way home again.

Thursday 29th May

I have always accepted that if you fill your window with rubbish, you can't complain if all the public offers to sell you is Mills and Boon paperbacks. If you want to buy better books, you should put something decent in the window, and at least pretend that they're the type of books you know something about.

In the past week, all that I've managed to buy is a collection of eight hundred Mills and Boons, and a book from Sam entitled 'A Short Introduction to the History of Human Stupidity'. It is 574 pages long. 'Pain in the Arse' tells me he is going to wait for the longer version to turn up.

I abandon the habits of a lifetime, fill my window with the leather bound sets that I've been storing at home, and wait hopefully. I do not have to wait long. The theory proves an immediate success: the Mills and Boon that I'm offered as a consequence are of a noticeably higher quality than those I was being offered before. I alter my sign to - MILLS AND BOON ~~25p~~ 35p - shut the front door behind me, and head for Bloomsbury.

James is already viewing the books when I arrive: Michael is conspicuous by his absence. I sense a look of disappointment on the auctioneer's face, when he sees that 'the man who bought the John Morley set' will not be attending today's sale.

I quickly succeed in purchasing an eighteenth century book on opium and a couple of volumes of archaelogical interest. I can't, for the life of me, understand what it is about the latter purchase that James finds so highly amusing.

The only other lot I buy is a nineteenth century volume of topographical engravings. It is what is known as a 'breaker', i.e. a book which is broken up for the illustrations it contains.

Bookbreaking is a practice which has split the booktrade into two opposing moral camps -

1. Dealers who consider that it's morally acceptable to break books and who proceed to make a lot of money by doing so.
2. Dealers who consider that it's morally wrong to break books (and who proceed to make money by doing it anyway).

I've never made any money from breakers because, whenever I've tried to buy them in the past, a certain member of the Crawley ring has outbid me. It's always struck me as ironic that he's the very dealer who has a sign in his shop which reads - BOOKBREAKERS NOT WELCOME.

When one considers that he probably makes more money out of breakers than any other dealer in the South of England, it's a little like Bernard Matthews putting up a sign in his factory reading - PRESERVE POULTRY.

I decide that the best way to make money from the book is to break it myself. Only when the razor blade is poised above the first engraving, does my resolve desert me. Why do we treat books with more respect than other objects? I have heard of chain saw serial killers who have broken down in tears because they have accidently ripped a page of their library book.

I am also put off by Dick coming in at that exact moment and assaulting me with his Harry Enfield impersonation.

"It's only me. I wouldn't do that if I were you. I wouldn't break that book. That's not a good book to break. It would take you years to sell those engravings. I wouldn't break that book if I were you."

I put down the razor blade and hand him the two volumes of archaelogical interest. Dick laughs uproariously.

I ignore him, and point out the curious fact that the last third of one of the books consists of blank pages. Dick points out that, carefully concealed within each pair of blank pages, is an engraving.

Each engraving depicts an oversized penis.

The two books, I am informed, are on the history of phallic worship. Despite being someone who comes out in hot flushes picking up a copy of the 'Sunday Sport' in my local newsagents, I have managed to outbid the entire London booktrade for books illustrated with pictures of mens' grotesquely enlarged private parts. I may not have known what I was doing but, judging by James' laughter, the rest of the booktrade did.

If Michael is to be known for evermore in Bloomsbury as the man for John Morley, I will be known as the man for big cocks.

There really is nothing else for it; I open the book at one of the more exaggerated illustrations and place it in the window.

Let's see what the ladies who persist in offering me Mills and Boon paperbacks make of that.

Sunday 9th June

The collection of books beneath my desk has grown in size, and has so far cost me £520. I give the remaining five pounds to the man from the fish and chip shop - for an Agatha Christie first in dustwrapper - and set about the business of disposing of my purchases.

There has been little movement in the penises in the window, other than a slight curling up at the edges where the sun is beginning to have an effect.

Reaction to them has diminished since the first day, when I found more old ladies gathered outside my shop than the Post Office gets on pension morning. All I get now is the odd old dear muttering "disgusting, disgusting" to herself as she strives to wipe the dust from the shop window.

Robert gives me £25 for the Agatha Christie, and I make a profit of a pound on my Chinese purchases, because Trevor takes pity on the more distressed of the volumes and takes it away to his sanctuary for battered books.

I leave for my weekly excursion to the bootsales, convinced that my experiment is making satisfactory progress. The bootsales are an unmitigated disaster. I head towards Ashford, because George has told me about a bootsale that is advertised as having 'BOOKS, BOOKS, BOOKS' for sale. I really should know better.

I drive to Ashford, and ask a local resident for directions to the sale. He tells me the quickest way is to follow the signs for Maidstone, get on the motorway, leave at the first exit, and re-enter Ashford from that direction. I do as he tells me; get on the motorway, and find that the first exit I come to is just outside Maidstone. By the time I arrive at the bootsale, the 'BOOKS, BOOKS, BOOKS' have all gone, gone, gone.

The great consolation of bootsales is that I usually manage to come away with something for the children. This morning, I buy an unbelievably loud football rattle, and an ancient device for practising golf which consists of a golf ball attached to a length of elastic and several metal pegs. There are no instructions in the box, the outide of which bears the guarantee -

THE BALL CANNOT HIT YOU WHEN IT RETURNS.

The look my wife gives me, on hearing the rattle, is the one she reserves for relatives who buy the children noisy drums for Christmas. I leave the house, golf club in hand, children in tow (rattling loudly), in the direction of the playing fields.

I have never been mechanically inclined. The pattern in which I arrange the pegs and elastic gives no indication of any mathematical premeditation. I place the ball on a tee, and stand back as my eleven year old prepares to take a swipe at it.

The ball, once struck, flies skyward, pulling the elastic behind it. It stops abruptly about twenty yards away, and returns along the path it has just travelled, striking my eleven year old son solidly on the forehead.

It is a blow that will, in all probability, be enough to put him off golf for life. I can only assume it's a golf device that was invented by someone of Australian/Irish extraction. Whoever invented it - I doubt very much if they made their fortune from it.

I return to work and my own attempt to make a fortune.

I sell the breaker to Dick (at a loss), and the book on opium to someone pretending to be a doctor. My £525 increases hesitantly to £565, and the only books I am unable to shift are the penis books, now noticeably showing signs of wilting in the intermittent summer sunlight.

I pocket the money, and pull from my desk drawer an application form for the Bohemia Road window display competition. I fill the space in the window with a selection of the novels of Jeffrey Archer, and the space on the application form for 'Theme of Display' with *'BIG PRICKS OF THE WORLD'*.

If I don't get a 'highly commended' this year, then I don't suppose that I ever shall.

Friday 28th June

Plan D - WORK WITHOUT A PLAN - is proving a bit too restrictive. I need a new plan. The first alternative that I consider for Plan E is -

WAIT UNTIL SOMEONE LEAVES ME BOOKS WORTH £565 IN THEIR WILL.

It is every bookdealer's dream to be left a collection of books by a grateful customer. In eleven years, I have received only one mention in a customer's will.

Most of the books that I sell are such rubbish, I would be absolutely horrified to have them offered back to me. Tom's books, however, were of a somewhat higher quality.

Tom was a regular. Early in our relationship he made a point of letting me know - "I've mentioned you in my will."

For the next seven or eight years I saved him most of the decent antiquarian books that came my way. My reasoning was simple: if I sold a book to Tom, I would get it back when he died and be able to make another profit on it. Usually I gave him a generous discount.

When Tom died, I was indeed mentioned in his will. The relevant passage read - *DON'T SELL MY BOOKS TO CLIVE LINKLATER.*

His will went on to explain that I sold books so cheaply, the relatives would almost certainly make more money if they offered his library to a more upmarket bookshop.

I decide that, because of the limited time available to me, I should consider alternatives for Plan E. The alternative I settle on is -

PESTER MR CROUCH SO MUCH HE EVENTUALLY GIVES IN AND SELLS ME SOME BOOKS FOR £565.

Plan E is successful more quickly than I could possibly have dreamt. For the next four days my conversation with Mr Crouch conforms to a consistent pattern.

"I've got £565 to spend and, if you're lucky, I might just spend it with you."

"Piss off."

On the fifth day, Mr Crouch cracks.

"I've got £565 to spend and, if you're lucky, I might just spend it with you."

"I'm meant to say that."

"So you are. I'm getting a bit confused. Piss off then."

On the sixth day, Mr Crouch cracks even more.

"I've got £565 to spend and, if you're lucky, I might just spend it with you."

"Aaaaaaaaaargh!" (the sound of a man cracking if ever there was one). "I've got an antiquarian book on comets you can have for £1,000".

I'm so delighted with the success of Plan E that it is several minutes before it dawns on me that I haven't got £1,000. I now have to think of what I need to do to get me from £565 to £1,000. Almost immediately, I know exactly what I need to do. What I need to do is think of Plan D (Part 2).

Easier said than done. I can't for the life of me think what Plan D (Part 2) should be. My first reaction is that it should read -

PANIC.

My second reaction is that it should combine all the best advice that I've received in the last few months, and read -

TAKE YOUR TIME, BE PATIENT, SPEND YOUR MONEY WISELY.

The version of Plan D (Part 2) that I finally decide upon reads -

TAKE YOUR TIME, BE PATIENT, SPEND YOUR MONEY WISELY (AND PANIC OCCASIONALLY).

The idea behind Plan D (Part 2) is that I should avoid rushing to the auctions and squandering my money yet again. I now have as much confidence in auctions, as a man who's been savaged by a miniature poodle has in pit bull terriers.

Plan D (Part 2) means I am now going to spend my £565 as carefully as possible; I am going to make a list of my purchases in the 'Bookdealer'; I am going to hope that the proceeds amount to £1,000; I am then going to buy the book on comets from Mr Crouch.

I settle back to await developments in an experiment that is coming to play an increasingly important role in my life.

The first person to offer me books is a nervous young lady

who wishes to sell a child's Bible and an Oxford edition of the Works of Shakespeare. Inside each volume is the same inscription -

'To Patrick, on your christening, 1988.'

I unintentionally give the lady a quizzical look.

"They were my son's. He died."

I offer her three pounds, and she leaves my shop with her dead son's christening presents still tucked under her arm.

Every so often, life has a habit of reminding us that most of what we do isn't that important after all.

Sunday 30th June

The worst thing about Sunday mornings is that they follow so quickly after Saturday nights. Even after fifteen years of marriage, Saturday nights are special.

As soon as my wife moves into her now familiar seduction routine, I know that she isn't about to let me down.

"YAWN. YAWN. I suppose because it's Saturday night you're going to want it again. YAWN. YAWN."

"Yes please - if it isn't too much trouble."

The secret of a successful marriage is variation. My wife is an expert at variation. Most weeks she varies the frequency and positioning of her yawns. Some weeks she actually pretends to fall asleep in the middle of her seduction routine. One week she really did fall asleep in the middle of her seduction routine, and I couldn't for the life of me find a way to wake her up.

My own search for variation is currently an attempt to persuade my wife to talk dirty. Last night provided the first indication that her inhibitions are beginning to break down. At her moment of greatest pleasure, she looked upwards and cried out at the top of her voice, "Oh, my goodness, oh, my goodness, oh, my goodness, just look at all those cobwebs on the ceiling."

This particular Sunday morning, I get out of bed at 5.30 and head for Chessington. I head for Chessington because there's an antiques fair being held there that is advertised as having space for 400 stalls.

I could do with looking at 400 antique stalls, because Plan D (Part 2), with it's laid back approach, is in need of some gentle encouragement. It is a plan that is already proving to have its advantages: less pressure, less stress. It is a plan that is also proving to have its disadvantages: less books. So far, to be precise: no books. If ever I felt a temptation to panic, I feel it now.

You can tell how advanced summer is by the number of multicoloured 'SUMMER FETE' notices that are flapping, rain-drenched, from the roadside tree trunks. I arrive at the Chessington antiques fair, to discover there are indeed spaces for 400 stalls; 4 of the spaces are occupied. I am beginning to realise that I have yet to master all the nuances of 'antique speak.'

I spend sixty pence and drive home through Guildford. Why I drive through Guildford, I have no idea. It takes me eighty miles out of my way. By the time I get to Bexhill, I have driven a total of two hundred miles. At this rate of progress, spending my £565 will involve me working for three years and driving 200,000 miles.

"Don't panic. Don't panic," I tell myself.

I discover an antiques fair in Bexhill (5 miles from Hastings) that provides me with eight pounds worth of books, and conclusive evidence that Law 6 of bookselling is indeed correct. Law 6 reads -

*THE FURTHER YOU TRAVEL LOOKING FOR BOOKS, THE
LESS LIKELY YOU ARE TO FIND ANY.*

I arrive home wet, bedraggled, and so exhausted that there isn't a part of my body with any feeling left in it. I open the front door to find my wife hoovering in the hallway and talking to herself as she does so - "Oh, my goodness. Oh, my goodness. Dust everywhere."

Imperceptibly almost, I notice the feeling returning to my loins.

Tuesday 16th July

I am a wiser man now than I was nine months ago. I have learnt, amongst other things, that it is probably easier to lose money in the auction room than it is to make it. I have learnt that the further you travel looking for books, the less likely you are to find any.

At seven o'clock in the morning, I set out to drive the sixty miles to the John Denman auction in Horsham. I have yet to learn how to stop myself from doing stupid things.

My new-found wisdom means that I have at least taken certain precautions. I have checked the auction advertisements in 'Antiques Trade Gazette' to make sure there is some mention of books. Sure enough, 'Books' is written with a capital B; an encouraging sign if ever I saw one. I have even phoned up to check there will be sufficient time to view the 'Books' on the morning of the sale.

"There will be if you come early; there's a lot to look through."

I arrive to be greeted by the usual array of auction lots: furniture, jewellery, porcelain....Only one category proves difficult to locate. Books. I ask the young man behind the glass cabinet where I can find them.

"Books?" he replies, staring at me blankly and open-mouthed.

I assume he's mentally subnormal in some way (he probably assumes the same of me), and I continue with my search. I do not for one moment doubt that the books are there somewhere. They were advertised as being in the sale; I was assured over the phone they would be in the sale. But where?

I search everywhere: behind cupboards, under armchairs, inside chamberpots. I pay two pounds for a catalogue, in the belief that, once I know the appropriate lot numbers, the books will suddenly become visible.

The catalogue is like the auction room. Devoid of books. For the first time I begin to have my doubts. I approach the auctioneer.

"Could you possibly point me in the direction of the books?"

161

"There aren't any."

"But you mentioned books in your advert. With a capital B."

"We always do."

"But I was told over the phone you had books."

"He was probably reading from the advert."

"But he gave me the impression there were lots of books."

"That's probably because it was written with a capital B."

I glare at the auctioneer in a manner intended to convey the message that I'm a potentially violent man. The auctioneer looks nervous. I give a big sigh and politely ask for a refund on my catalogue. The auctioneer looks relieved and gives me back my two pounds.

I drive home a wiser man. (I stop at Haywards Heath and pick up an unusually intelligent hitchhiker.) I now know for sure that there are certain aspects of 'antique speak' that will forever be beyond my comprehension.

Despite this particular disaster, Plan D (Part 2) is proving something of a success. I am taking my time; I am being patient; I am spending my money wisely. Only very occasionally am I panicking. My £565 is steadily being transformed into a small collection of interesting books.

I am buying a few books privately. I am buying a few books at auction. Mostly, though, I am buying by making sure that I am the first person to see all the fresh stock that turns up in the local bookshops. When Sam arrives for work in the morning, I am there waiting. When Michael arrives for work in the morning, I am there waiting. When James arrives for work in the morning, I am there waiting. This is quite an achievement on my part, as Sam, Michael and James all arrive for work at the same time and their shops are all some distance apart. It's a method that enables me to spend £300 of my money, with every prospect of spending more at the Ardingly Summer Antique Fair.

I know that the Ardingly Fair is approaching when a large poster appears in Reg Marley's shop window. It reads -

CHEAP DAY TRIPS TO ARDINGLY ANTIQUES FAIR. Presumably he's having to advertise because of sales resistance from his regulars. At the bottom of the poster, someone has scribbled - 'in luxury air-conditioned wardrobe'. I hurry past.

I have already resigned myself to paying the £35 entrance fee, when Clem Shankly, one of my regulars, comes up with a suggestion.

"I've got a ticket. Perhaps you'd like to try and forge it."

He agrees to leave the ticket with me for a couple of hours and I set to work. The task is simpler than I'd imagined. The ticket is a star-shaped, maroon piece of card; the task of forgery could not be easier. By the time I have finished it, it is virtually impossible to tell the copy from the original. Clem Shankly is impressed. He grabs his ticket and says he'll look out for me at Ardingly.

The things we do to save a bit of money. The closer I get to the entrance to Ardingly Antiques Fair, the more apprehensive I become. It reminds me of the bus journeys I took as a child when I would try and get away without paying. I used to spend the entire journey quivering like a nervous wreck in case an inspector got on at the next stop and threw me off the bus. It hardly seemed worth it.

My fears today prove totally unfounded. I am ushered past by the gateman, who gives no more than a cursory glance at my ticket.

There are few surprises waiting for me inside the antiques fair. The usual overpriced crap. The usual rival booksellers who always seem to arrive at the boxes of books just before I do. The only thing that does surprise me is that I am unable to find Clem Shankly in order to thank him.

I buy three books. One of them is a book of Bartlett engravings, worth £60, which I buy for a pound. I am approaching the exit when, if I'm not mistaken, I hear the voice of Clem Shankly. It is a voice which, if I'm not mistaken, is somewhat agitated. He appears to be shouting.

"How many times do I have to tell you: this ticket is not a forgery."

I turn the corner to be greeted by the sight of Clem Shankly being carried through the exit gate by two burly security guards. He catches sight of me in the distance.

"He's the one. He's the one with the forged ticket," he

screams, pointing in my direction.

The two guards turn towards me, but by the time they have done so, I am already hiding inside Reg Marley's wardrobe.

Sunday 21st July

I am continually stressing to my children the importance of choosing a good career. Mostly, though, I stress the importance of choosing a career which they will enjoy.

"You mean to say you enjoy getting up at 5 o'clock in the morning to go to bootsales?" observes my eleven year old son.

It is a remark, I feel, which fully warrants the clip round the ear that he receives for making it.

When I enter the Brighton bootsale at 5.45 in the morning, I have the £200 remaining from my £565, and no doubt whatsoever that it will be more than sufficient to pay for my morning's purchases. I am about to be proved mistaken.

I pay £100 for a collection of Lionel Edwards books, before discovering a copy of Wrights 'Illustrated Book of Poultry' on the floor beneath another stall. It is a book I recently saw auctioned in London for several hundred pounds. The price being asked for today's copy is £100. I hesitate and walk away. The reason I do so is because of Law 7 of bookselling which reads -

THE PRICES REALISED BY BOOKS AT AUCTION BEAR LITTLE OR NO RELATION TO THE BOOKS' TRUE VALUE

In theory, the price achieved by a book at auction is a result of competitive bidding by the various people who are interested in buying it. Nothing could be further from the truth.

The price of a book at auction is far more likely to be arrived at in one of the following ways -

1) SOMEONE BIDDING FOR THE WRONG LOT

At every auction, a percentage of lots must inevitably be sold to people who weren't in the least bit interested in buying them in the first place. The only person who knows when this happens is the one who has to pay for them. In next year's Book Auction Records will be an entry - JOHN MORLEY-Complete works (De Luxe Edition) £45. Bookdealers up and down the country will see this, comment, "I see John Morley's fetching money now," and go rushing round their shops increasing the prices on all the John Morley items that they've had in stock for the last twenty five years. Perhaps Wrights 'Poultry' sold in London to someone who wasn't even aware that was the lot they were bidding on.

2) AUCTIONEER PRETENDING THAT A BOOK HAS SOLD WHEN IT HASN'T

In every auction, there will be books that don't sell. In an honest world, the auctioneer would announce, "Well, that was a pretty crappy book. I'm not in the least bit surprised that no one wanted to buy it." In the real world, the auctioneer will pretend that it's sold by calling out the name of a ficticious buyer. Most auctioneers have their own pet names which they use in this situation. It was quite a while before I realised that the 'Mr Conmans' and the 'Mr Cheaters', who appeared to buy so frequently, did not in fact exist. Perhaps the Wrights 'Poultry' that I thought I saw sell in London didn't actually sell at all.

3. THE PRESENCE OF A NUTTER IN THE AUCTION ROOMS

Many books are put in auction with a reserve that far exceeds the true value of the book. In theory, for this book to sell, it is necessary for a couple of nutters to bid against each other until the reserve is passed. In practice, one nutter will suffice. In this situation, the auctioneer will take bids 'off the wall' until the reserve is reached and the nutter can go home with his book. If there is no nutter in the room (an unsual situation), the auctioneer will take bids 'off opposite walls' so that he can pretend to sell the book at the level of it's grossly inflated reserve. Perhaps it was a nutter who bought the Wrights 'Poultry' in London.

4. THE PRESENCE OF AN OWNER NUTTER IN THE AUCTION ROOM

Some people who put books into auction actually attend

REFLECTIONS FROM A BOOKSHOP WINDOW

the sale and bid for their own books, in an attempt to make some other nutter pay more for the books than they would otherwise have had to. Occasionally these owner nutters get so carried away, they end up buying back their own books. It's just possible that the buyer of Wrights 'Poultry' in London was simply an owner nutter buying back his own book.

5. THE PRESENCE OF TWO IGNORANT NUTTERS IN THE AUCTION ROOM

At the recent Hornsey auction, there was an ignorant nutter who believed that a three volume set of 'Masterpieces of British Art' was valuable. It happened that, in the room that day, was another ignorant nutter who believed the same thing. The two nutters bid fiercely against each other, until ignorant nutter Mark I went home rejoicing having bought the books for £80. Ignorant nutter Mark II went home broken-hearted. What neither of them realised is that 'Masterpieces of British Art' is a set you can pick up in any bookshop in the country for a fiver. Maybe Wrights 'Poultry' was fought over in London by a couple of ignorant nutters.

6. THE PRESENCE OF GREEDY NUTTERS IN THE AUCTION ROOM

There are certain nutters who are less concerned with buying books than they are with stopping anyone else in the room having them. Put two of these greedy nutters in the same auction and you have a confrontation that ultimately no one can win. A couple of years ago, a book auction was held in Battle where about twenty greedy nutters all turned up at the same time. A lot of bookdealers lost a lot of money as a result of their purchases on that particular day. Perhaps the Wrights 'Poultry' in London was bought by a greedy nutter simply to stop anybody else buying it.

All things considered, it's hardly surprising that I have my doubts about paying £100 for Wrights 'Poultry', even though I apparently saw another copy sell for several hundred pounds just a few weeks ago.

I turn my back on the book, and prepare to continue my tour of the Brighton bootsale. I walk twenty yards, change my mind, and return to find another bookdealer examining the book that, all of a sudden, I am desperately keen to buy.

After several anxious minutes, my rival puts the book down and walks away for about three paces, before turning and attempting to retrieve the book that he has just released from his grasp.

By the time he has done so, I am lying on top of it.

For three weeks, I have gone about disposing of my £565 by taking my time, by being patient, and by spending my money wisely. I now manage to dispose of the last one hundred pounds in a moment of sheer blind panic.

The true value of Wrights 'Poultry' could well determine whether I am able to sell my £565 worth of purchases for the magic £1,000.

As soon as I return home, I look it up in Book Auction Records. A copy sold in 1903 for 15s. James tells me over the phone that ten years ago it was selling for sixty pounds.

"And last year?" I enquire anxiously.

"Five hundred pounds, consistently"

I get the feeling I might just have done rather well.

Saturday 27th July

Law 8 of secondhand bookselling reads -
MOST BOOKS THAT ENTER THE SECONDHAND
BOOKTRADE NEVER LEAVE IT.
Occasionally a book will escape into the library of a private collector; mostly, though, books are fated to be passed forever from the hands of one secondhand bookdealer into the hands of another.

In the latest Bloomsbury catalogue is an entry that reads -
LOT 152. CARADOC, OF LLANCARFAN. THE
HISTORIE OF CAMBRIA, NOW CALLED WALES.

The description of faults that follows defines this copy, unmistakably, as the same copy I bought at Sevenoaks and subsequently sold to Nick Bernstein. It is now, it seems, about to embark on the next stage of it's journey towards the Black Hole Bookshop.

For other books, the journey is not quite so straightforward.

Robert recently disposed of a quantity of surplus stock, at ten pence a volume, to Sam. Amongst them was a book on trees that, three years earlier, Robert had bought from Sam for six pounds.

Sam reasoned that if he could sell it once, he could do so again, and placed it on his shelves priced once more at six pounds.

It sold three days later.

To Robert.

Now there is a book which may never reach the Black Hole Bookshop. It seems destined to spend its days passing backwards and forwards from Sam to Robert and then back again.

I have never seen Sam so happy as when he related this particular episode to me. Perhaps it will inspire him to produce more notices. The only recent addition to the display reads -
THE CUSTOMER IS ALWAYS RIGHT (EXCEPT
IN HERE).
George is also in a bouyant mood. A letter has been published in this week's Hastings Observer describing how rude he is to the foreign students that enter his shop. He has cut the letter out and stuck it in his window. He has become a hero among local bookdealers.

169

The letter goes on to describe how polite James is to the same students. None of the local bookdealers are talking to James.

I make my way home and, now that my £565 is spent, the prospect of preparing my Bookdealer list. It is not a job to which I am particularly looking forward. Two things worry me about listing books in the Bookdealer.

1. It's hard work

2. I might make a mistake.

Misprice a book in your shop, and only the dealer who buys it will ever know. Misprice a book in the Bookdealer, and overnight you can become the laughing stock of the entire secondhand booktrade.

You will not, though, be alone in your moment of humiliation. Three weeks ago, a list appeared advertising a set of twelve Far Eastern books for sale at £130. Mr Crouch sold his last set for £8,000. By the time Mr Crouch phoned up in the evening, the seller had long since taken his phone off the hook.

I think that serves Mr Crouch right. I still remember the occasion he found a £650 book in a Bohemia Road antique shop, priced at one pound fifty. He then haggled until he got the price reduced to a pound. I like to think Mr Crouch is now being made to suffer for his past meanness.

I reluctantly pick up my pen, and I am about to begin my list when the telephone rings. It's Mike Cassidy and he's been talking to James.

"I hear you've picked up a Wrights 'Poultry'; any chance of seeing it?"

He gives me £450 for the Wrights (which has 3 plates missing), £200 for the Lionel Edwards collection, and £60 for the Bartlett book that I bought for a pound at Ardingly.

In all, he spends £830 on books which cost me £230. I suddenly find that the entire nature of my experiment has been radically altered, mainly as a result of a single visit to a Brighton bootsale. I am left with books that cost me £335, and the knowledge that I am already very close to my £1,000 target. I abandon all thought of a list in the Bookdealer, and invite the local dealers to inspect my remaining stock.

I sell James the books that I bought from Sam; George the

books that I bought from Michael; and Robert the books that I bought from James. They all seem happy enough. I then reduce the price of the remaining books until I'm selling them for less than I paid for them.

In no time at all they are gone. In a state of some excitement, I add up my takings. The total comes to £1,448. I give myself a small round of applause.

I can now go to Mr Crouch and say those magic words.

"I've got £1,448 to spend and, if you're lucky, I might just spend it with you."

It will be interesting to see what Mr Crouch's reaction is to that.

Wednesday 31st July

"I've got £1,448 to spend and, if you're lucky, I might just spend it with you."

"Come on in then and see what you think of this book on comets."

What I think of 'this book on comets' is that it is remarkably small. Indeed, I would go so far as to say ridiculously small for a book that is supposed to be worth £1,000. In my mind, I had an image of a book that would require the assistance of a forklift truck to raise it from the ground. I try to hide my disappointment.

"And you want a thousand for it?"

"In cash."

I can see already that Mr Crouch is not going to be an easy man to deal with.

"And supposing I can't sell it?"

"I'll give you your money back."

"And supposing I haven't got the thousand on me?"

"You can take the book anyway."

"And supposing I manage to lose the book?"

"That would be my loss."

He's a tough negotiator this Mr Crouch, but I do believe I'm getting the better of him.

Mr Crouch bought the book twenty years ago from a man in Turkey. It cost him £60. The title page reads -

THEATRUM COMETICUM - Lubieniecki 1666

It is, by all accounts, the classic 17th century work on comets. I tuck it under my arm and set out for London, having promised to return with either the book or the money.

I'm a great fan of the *SELLING A BOOK BEFORE YOU BUY IT TECHNIQUE,* but this seems almost too good to be true.

I decide that, before I get on the train, I ought to at least try and dress like someone who owns a thousand pound book. I ask my wife where she keeps my other clothes.

"You haven't got any," she informs me.

That solves that problem. I head for Sothebys.

Sothebys tell me they would be happy to auction the book - in December. I head for Christies. Christies tell me they would be delighted to auction it - at the end of October. I only have until October 8th. I head for Quaritches.

Even Sam could learn something from Quaritches. The front door is locked and you have to ring the bell to gain admittance. I expect the door to be opened by a wizened old man. I am greeted instead by a cheerful youth.

He seems even more cheerful having seen the book. He calls for a colleague to take a look. I wait expectantly for the wizened old man. A skinhead arrives.

Between them they study the book in great detail. A Latin inscription on the title page causes great merriment. I ask to be let in on the joke. The inscription apparently translates -

'Major should stand down and give way to the majority parties'.

You can tell you're in Quaritches because all the jokes they make are in Latin. They offer me £1,500, and tell me it's a book that would be perfect for exhibiting at the Los Angeles Book Fair.

As their thoughts drift off to Los Angeles book fairs, I find myself thinking of Bexhill bootsales.

I pocket their cheque and walk out into the crowded London streets.

All of a sudden, I find that I have £1,948 to spend, and a growing awareness that there may, after all, be money to be made from secondhand books.

Good old Mr Crouch.

Monday 5th August

"I've got £1,948 to spend and, if you're lucky, I might just spend it with you," is the greeting I give to anyone who is unfortunate enough to drift within earshot.

If there is no one there to listen, I repeat it endlessly to myself.

My speech, I notice, is becoming slurred and hesitant; my head is spinning. I feel as though I am on a roundabout that is turning faster and faster. I feel as though I would quite like to get off.

I know what I need. A new plan certainly. Mostly, though, I need a holiday. I jot down a list of possible destinations -

1) A month in Bali.
2) A fortnight at Disneyworld.
3) A long weekend at Butlins.

It is not a decison I can take alone. My family is run on democratic lines. I duplicate the list and hand a copy to each of the voters.

"Where the hell's Bali?" demands my twenty month old daughter, whose vocabulary has come on remarkably in the last eight weeks.

After due consideration (and a gentle nudge from her brothers), she casts her vote for Disneyworld. Voting is by proportional representation. Each family member is allocated votes according to their seniority. Ben has two votes, Simon four, Stephen eight, my wife sixteen. All choose Disneyworld. Total votes for Disneyworld, 31.

Five faces turn expectantly in my direction. I do not hesitate. I cast my votes for Butlins: all 32 of them. Total votes for Butlin's, 32.

"It's Butlin's again this year," I announce to the waiting electorate.

"Damn," exclaims my wife. "I really thought we'd got it this time."

For years my wife produced children in the belief that, once she had enough of them, it would enable her to go on the holiday of her choice.

"There's always next year," I console her, as I open out the road map to Bognor Regis.

Now all I need is a plan. My advisers insist it should be a variation of Plan E and read -

PESTER MR CROUCH SO MUCH, HE EVENTUALLY GIVES IN AND SELLS ME SOME BOOKS FOR £1,948.

I feel, on reflection, that my experiment has already placed more than enough demands on the good will of Mr Crouch. I need to use my imagination. My imagination comes up with a Plan F which reads -

TAKE YOUR TIME, BE PATIENT, SPEND YOUR MONEY WISELY, (PANIC OCCASIONALLY), AND VISIT THE BRIGHTON BOOTSALE AS FREQUENTLY AS POSSIBLE.

I have never been renowned for the power of my imagination.

It is soon apparent that there is a limit to the number of times you can visit the Brighton bootsale. That limit is once a week. It is soon apparent that there is a limit to the number of times you can be incredibly lucky at the Brighton bootsale. That limit is once.

My next two visits to the Brighton bootsale do not produce a single book. My only purchase is half a dozen free range eggs, from the stall where a fortnight earlier I had discovered Wrights 'Poultry'.

Out of habit almost, I continue my rounds of the local bookshops. After a couple of circuits, I have almost forgotten what it is I'm looking for. I am in George's, when a customer approaches his desk.

"I'm looking for a book. Have you got it?"

"Which book?"

"I can't remember."

I am beginning to know exactly how he feels.

It is now clear that a plan which enabled me to spend £500 is not a suitable plan for spending £2,000. I hastily abandon Plan F in favour of Plan G.   Plan G reads -

PRAY

It gives every appearance of being the last desperate plan of a desperate man. My prayers are not private ones. They consist of display ads which I take out in the classified sections of virtually every paper in south east England.

What I would like to write is -

PLEASE, PLEASE, PLEASE, SOMEBODY SELL ME BOOKS FOR £2,000

What I do in fact write is -

BOOKS BOUGHT

Followed by my telephone number.

I then sit by the phone to see if my prayers are about to be answered.

Tuesday 13th August

There has been no response whatsoever to my advertisements in the paper. Out of the first ten phonecalls I receive, five are from double glazing salesmen, one is from my five year old son practising his telephone dialling technique, and four are from friends of mine pretending to be J.R. Hartley.

I can't remember the last time a friend phoned me up without pretending to be J.R. Hartley. I know it isn't J.R. Hartley the moment they ask if I've got a copy of 'Fly Fishing'. It's common knowledge, within the booktrade, that the real J.R. Hartley is now phoning round all the bookshops in Yellow Pages trying to sell the damn thing.

I am gradually becoming resigned to the feeling that my experiment may not progress beyond the figure of £1,948.

There are many people, no doubt, who would consider this to be a perfectly acceptable moment to abandon the whole project.

They, of course, would not belong to a family whose motto is 'Persevere boy'.

They, of course, would not have been there to see Wilson's willy.

It has always been an inspiration to me that I was witness to the greatest example of human perseverance ever seen. A spider may have inspired Robert the Bruce to try, try and try again; but my inspiration has always been the memory of Wilson's willy.

However tempted I may feel to give up at this moment, I only have to cast my mind back to that fateful evening, conjure up a mental picture of Wilson's willy, and it gives me the determination to carry on.

Wilson was a sixth form schoolfriend. On the evening of the school sports heats, he wore his new, bright, red shorts for the first time. I had, of course, seen him run many times before and, as soon as the race started, I recognised his familiar stride pattern to the first hurdle. By the time he thrust his left leg over the hurdle, he was already, as usual, well clear of the field.

As his leading leg cleared the hurdle and returned to the track, I expected him to resume his rythmic athletic running. Even from a distance, though, I could see that something was seriously wrong. His normal smooth stride had become stuttering and chaotic, his hands fumbled at the front of his shorts, and he was halfway towards the next hurdle before his composure returned.

From my trackside position, I concentrated my gaze as he approached the next hurdle; the final extended stride, the left leg thrust up and over the hurdle, the willy emerging from the front of Wilson's new shorts.

As Wilson sailed over the second hurdle, a part of Wilson's anatomy which any well designed pair of shorts would have kept restrained, became unrestrained. As Wilson flew over the second hurdle as free as a bird, so did his willy.

I rubbed my eyes in disbelief. Again on landing, the same disjointed stride pattern, the same frantic fumbling with his hands as Wilson endeavoured to stuff his flailing member back within the confines of his shorts.

The stride count, which should have brought Wilson to the next hurdle at the count of eight, seemed neverending.......43, 44, 45; again the left leg thrusting up and over, again the willy popping almost apologetically from the opening at the front of Wilson's shorts.

It was by now clear that there was some law of nature that, combining the exertion of hurdling and the design of Wilson's shorts, meant that as surely as Wilson thrust out his left leg, so surely was his willy bound to follow.

To this day, I still have this image in my mind, of Wilson suspended almost motionless above a hurdle: left arm, left leg, willy, all pointing towards the finishing line.

I quote this incident as an example of perseverance because, surely, if ever there was a situation in which it would have been excusable to give up, this was it. If Wilson had stopped after the first hurdle, returned his willy to its natural habitat and walked to the side of the track, no one would have been any the wiser. Wilson, though, was no quitter. It is more a reflection on his fellow competitors, than a recommendation for his unique hurdling technique, that Wilson still managed to win the race.

The expression on Wilson's face was that of someone in the middle of a particularly bad nightmare. It was a nightmare that was not yet over.

"Boys, take your places for the semi-final heats," boomed the voice of the games master.

I am sure there have been murderers who have approached the gallows with more enthusiasm than Wilson approached the starting line.

What is it about a disaster that draws a crowd towards it? Why did the Girl Guides choose that moment to take a short cut across the school grounds? What caused the two old ladies, walking their dogs, to hesitate and watch?

Wilson's running took its now familiar pattern: the final extended stride, the thrust of the left leg, the emergence of the willy. Nobody said a word. It was almost as if they couldn't believe the evidence of their eyes.

For the record, Wilson won comfortably again. By the time he arrived at the finishing line, he had long since abandoned any pretence at decency. His policy by then was to get it all over as quickly as possible, and he moved swiftly through the latter part of the race with his willy protruding proudly before him.

As Wilson turned his back and headed for the changing rooms, there were sighs of disappointment from the Girl Guides who had watched open mouthed throughout. The two old ladies walked away somewhat shakily, forgetting to take their dogs with them.

In my opinion, for Wilson to have won those races on that now distant summer evening is the ultimate example of human perseverance. With Wilson as my inspiration, I really have no choice but to continue with my experiment to the bitter end.

Thursday 15th August

My thirteen year old son is beginning to develop a speech defect. He is unable to construct a sentence that doesn't have a reference to money in it. A typical father and son conversation might go -

FATHER: Morning son, looks like being a lovely day.

SON: It would be if I had a pair of Poser sunglasses.

FATHER: Nice day for a walk.

SON: Not without a pair of Rip off trainers.

Under normal circumstances, it is a conversation that I would have no difficulty in bringing to a satisfactory conclusion -

FATHER: Lend us a fiver, could you, son.

My problem now is that I have a couple of thousand pounds to spend, and a family who are only too aware of that fact.

My tactic so far has been to promise to buy them everything they ask for, provided they are prepared to wait until my experiment ends in October. My shopping list for the morning of October 8th reads -

WIFE: Three piece suite. (She tells me she has had enough of looking at bright purple furniture for the past twelve years. I tell her it's a colour I can't get enough of. She responds by buying me a pair of bright purple trousers for my birthday.)

13 YEAR OLD SON: Computer, mountain bike, television, video recorder, hi-fi system.

11 YEAR OLD SON: Set of golf clubs, crash helmet.

5 YEAR OLD SON: Packet of Maltesers. (He doesn't yet seem aware of the unique opportunity that is available to him.)

20 MONTH OLD DAUGHTER: Concise Oxford Dictionary.

I decide that, before the list gets any longer, I would be well advised to dispose of my £1,948 at the earliest available opportunity.

Reluctantly, I head back to the auctions.

I attend the sales in Hove and Canterbury and fail to buy a book. I study the catalogue for the forthcoming Bloomsbury sale with a sense of increased determination. Lot 248 reads -

ILLUSTRATED LONDON NEWS: 1842-1973. Incomplete set,
some duplicates. 247 volumes. Estimate £750-£1,000.

They're big, they're old, they're illustrated, and they would require a very large lorry to move them. I'm sorely tempted. I ask James' advice. He tells me he can't think of anything less interesting to spend my money on. I ask my wife's advice. She threatens to leave me if I buy them. I'm sorely tempted.

I can understand my wife's concern. For many years she has suffered from an acute case of foliophobia. According to the medical dictionary, this consists of -

'An irrational fear of being hit on the head by a large book falling
from a great height.'

It's an illness that stems from the time I was given a quarter of a million books by Guy, and my family had to spend two years living in a cupboard under the stairs, because the rest of the house was full up with books.

Its only to be expected that my wife should suffer a panic attack at the prospect of having 247 volumes of the Illustrated London News stored in her living room.

I consider my options carefully. This may be one of the only opportunities I get to spend my £1,948 before October 8th. I may, on the other hand, have terrible trouble finding another wife. It is not an easy decision to have to make.

Even by the time I walk through the door at Bloomsbury, I am still not convinced that I am doing the correct thing. The image of my wife standing in the doorway shouting - "If you buy those books, don't expect to find me here when you get back." - has haunted me throughout my journey.

I wait apprehensively for the bidding on Lot 248 to commence. It doesn't occur to me, for one moment, that £1,948 might be insufficient to purchase the lot. When I start to bid at £750, I smile at those around me as I bask in the glory of having such a vast fortune to dispose of. The girl from Quaritches smiles sympathetically back.

I am still smiling when I attempt, five minutes later, to slink unnoticed from the back of the saleroom. It is a smile that requires an enormous effort on my part to maintain. I don't imagine the other dealers are particularly impressed by a bookseller who stops bidding at £2,000, on a collection of books that eventually sell for £6,400.

I am almost out of the door when, out of the corner of my eye, I catch sight of the girl from Quaritch waving to me as I go. She could, of course, be bidding. (Not waving, but bidding. I must surely become famous for that sentence.)

As I walk towards the railway station, I weigh up the consequences of my failure.

On the negative side, I might find I now have no more realistic chances of disposing of my money.

On the positive side, I still have nearly £2,000 in my pocket. I still have a wife.

On balance, I decide that I probably have sufficient reason to whistle to myself as I walk in sunshine alongside the Thames.

Wednesday 28th August

However I choose to measure my experiment, I sense that it is rapidly drawing to a conclusion. Certainly there are still more days to be crossed off the calendar, more miles to be driven, more nods of the head to be made at auction. Certainly there is still enough time for yet another layer of dust to settle on Michael's complete set of the works of John Morley. There does, though, seem to be a dearth of opportunities for spending £2,000.

Ron Hodgson phones me up and (after a brief interlude where he pretends to be J.R. Hartley) enquires as to the progress of my experiment. I tell him of my incredible financial success. He tells me the story of a bookdealer who recently paid £30 for a manuscript which subsequently sold for £40,000. Perhaps my success isn't so incredible after all.

Driffield phones up and informs me he is about to publish his 'Guide to the Secondhand Bookshops of Britain'. He reads out the list for this area and asks me to verify its completeness. There is no mention of 'Sam's Emporium'. Driffield tells me that Sam is excluded because of his irregular opening hours. I tell Driffield that compiling a list of Hastings and Bexhill booksellers, without mentioning Sam, is like writing a book entitled 'Fat Men in British Politics' without mentioning Cyril Smith. I head to Sam's to break the bad news to him. I can't get in.

The barricades now erected outside 'Sam's Emporium' are as impenetrable as those which last week went up outside the Russian parliament. Just inside the shop, is a stolen no entry sign with the words 'DEALERS ONLY' written on it. In front of this is a barrier designed on the same principle as a level crossing gate. It is opened by potential customers pushing two lengths of wood upwards and outwards. Most customers never even reach this point. To do so, they have to negotiate a plank of wood which is suspended by two lengths of rope from the top of the shop (garage) doorway.

To enter 'Sam's Emporium', a customer thus has to hold a barrier above their head with one hand, while at the same time pushing a second barrier upwards and outwards with the other.

Anyone successful in achieving this is greeted by a notice

informing them they can't come in unless they're a dealer.

It's hardly surprising that the overall effect of this obstacle course on booklovers is the same as that which the Venus Flytrap has on flies. When I arrive, half a dozen little old ladies are stranded between the two barriers, with no obvious indication of which direction they're moving in.

"Why doesn't Sam want them in?" asks my thirteen year old son.

It's one of those questions to which there isn't an easy answer. We head for Michael's.

Perhaps the customer who follows us into Michael's sheds some light on Sam's contempt for the general public. Like all good booksearchers and double glazing salesmen, his opening sentence gives no indication that he is intent on wasting Michael's time.

"Have you got any pocket editions?"

"Hundreds of them." (I notice a glimmer of wetness around the corner of Michael's mouth.)

"Any Oxford Classics?"

"Scores of them."

"Any of them by Trollope?"

"Half a dozen of them."

"Is one of them called 'The Warden'?"

"I do believe one of them is."

"Thats marvellous. I've been looking for a copy of that for years. How much is it?"

"Fifty pence."

"Blimey, that's expensive. There's no way I'm paying that much. I'll wait until a cheaper copy turns up."

With that, he hurries out in the direction of 'Sam's Emporium, where the barricades are up and waiting.

The only chance to spend my money is at an auction of railway books in Worthing. I view the sale, and calculate that it would be theoretically possible to dispose of all my money there. There is, though, a problem. The problem is my wife.

The auction takes place on the middle day of our holiday. (Butlins was booked up, and we have settled on a midweek break at a holiday camp near Chichester.) I tell my wife that I may have to slip out for a couple of hours on the Wednesday morning. She tells me that, if I leave her to look after the children, she'll never go on holiday with me again. She puts me in something of a dilemma. It's a dilemma that worries me throughout the drive to Worthing.

My wife has never forgiven me for the first holiday we took at Butlins, when I spent the entire weekend watching Steve Davis playing Jimmy White in the world snooker final.

"Do you really mean to say," enquired my wife, "that you consider sitting in a darkened room with only a television to look at, more enjoyable than a holiday at Butlins?"

"I'd consider sitting in a pitch black room, without a television to look at, more enjoyable than a holiday at Butlins," came my reply.

I had not at that point been converted to the joys of a British holiday camp. For most people, the joys of Butlins are the glamorous knee contests and the knobbly granny competitions. For me, it's the moment in the week when a young lady in saucy underwear sits on your lap while the holiday camp photographer takes your picture.

I now spend the first half of my annual holiday looking forward to this moment, and the second half studying the photograph. (One year, I kept moving round the ballroom, and managed to get my photograph taken fourteen times in the same compromising position. I like to think that even the young lady was getting aroused by the end of it.)

On the journey to Worthing, when I'm not thinking about a holiday without my wife, I'm thinking about those fourteen photographs. Not once do I think about turning back.

It takes me an hour and a half to get to the auction. It takes me three minutes to learn that the railway books are going to be far too expensive for me to buy. I apprehensively set out on the journey back to Chichester.

By the time I get back, my two eldest children are beating each other to a pulp, and the two youngest have simultaneously developed an extremely bad case of diarrhoea. My wife is sitting in the middle of them sobbing her heart out. I make my excuses and head towards the photographer's shop.

Thursday 19th September

I never consider summer to be over until Hastings Town are knocked out of the F.A.Cup. I never have to wait too long. By my definition, summer is already over.

When I arrive at bootsales now, it is still dark; there is a chill in the air. I drag my feet out of dew soaked grass and put them down again in glistening cow pats. ("Going through the motions," as Michael describes it.)

I have now abandoned all thought of spending my £1,948. I do not, it seems, have sufficient time to dispose of it gradually. Fate, it seems, has no intention of putting a valuable library my way. It almost happened though.

Two weeks ago, George was offered a garage full of books in Canterbury for £2,000. He turned them down, on the grounds that it was too much like hard work. By the time he mentioned it to me, they had already been disposed of.

Apparently, they were subsequently offered to a Canterbury bookshop where the assistant wrote down the wrong phone number. The bookshop owner phoned back to say he was definitely interested, and found himself listening to a pre-recorded message entitled 'Inside my Gymslip'. Another bookshop assistant bites the dust.

Rumour has it they were bought by another Kent dealer, who got his money back on half a dozen breakers he found buried in a corner of the garage. Que sera sera.

I do, though, continue to be vigilant, in case fate shows any sign of bringing me a change of fortune.

Late one afternoon, a customer enquires if I have any 19th century colour plate books on heraldry. It is the first such enquiry I have had in three years. By amazing coincidence, Sam had been in half an hour earlier and offered me a 19th century colour plate book on heraldry. It is the first such book I had seen in three years. If that isn't fate at work, I don't know what is.

I tell the customer all about it.

"Would it be possible to have a look at it then?"

"I didn't buy it."

"Why the hell not?"

186

"Nobody ever asks me for 19th century colour plate books on heraldry."

I don't think there can be much doubt about the sort of future that fate has in store for me.

The choice that faces me is simple: keep the money, or gamble it in the auction rooms. It isn't really much of a choice at all. To spend it now at auction could ruin a year's hard work. I hide the money in the one place that even I would not want to go looking for it: the drawer where I keep my smelly socks.

The next day I take it to the building society. The young lady behind the desk takes the understandable precaution of holding the money up to the light, and the unusual precaution of passing the money under her nose. It is a decision she immediately regrets.

"Not counterfeit money, smelly feet money," I call after her as she rushes off in search of fresh air.

Sometimes the hardest thing to do in life is nothing. The next day I return to the building society and ask for my money back. They hand it over wrapped in a polythene bag. I couldn't cope with the thought of having nothing to do for two weeks, and I have decided to spend my money at the first available book auction.

The first available book auction is in Billingshurst at 2.00p.m. on Thursday. It is also in Sevenoaks at 2.00p.m. on Thursday. Whoever arranges these auctions should definitely apply for a job writing bus timetables. Having waited two months for a decent sale to turn up, two of them arrive together.

I view the Sevenoaks sale and leave bids totalling £1,700. I attend the Billingshurst sale prepared to bid up to £1,800. The greatest danger now is that I could end up spending more money than I have available.

I manage to spend £440 at Billingshurst, and I keep my fingers crossed that I have not spent more than £1,500 at Sevenoaks. I have, in fact, spent £89.

Nobody can accuse me of not keeping going to the bitter end. I now have a fortnight to try and get my money back on books that I immediately regret buying. Mr Crouch comes in and enquires how my experiment is going.

"I've got £1,419 to spend."

"Speak up. I can't hear you."

"I've got £1,419 to spend."

"And?"

"And, if you're lucky, I might just spend it with you."

"You've got £1,419 to spend and, if I'm lucky, you might just spend it with me."

I can tell from the tone of his voice, that I've become a major disappointment in Mr Crouch's eyes.

Tuesday 24th September

The most pleasant sound I know is the sound of raindrops falling on my window on a Sunday morning. It means I can stay in bed and don't have to get up and go to the bootsales.

It rains all day Sunday and all day Monday. It brightens up just in time for the Ardingly September Antiques Fair. I stand by the fair entrance in the hope that someone might sell me a spare ticket.

"Psst, sell me a ticket for a tenner," is the greeting I give to every stallholder who drives past. I am enjoying myself so much, it's something of an anticlimax when I do succeed in buying a ticket for ten pounds. It means that I have saved myself twenty five pounds.

"Thank you God," I say, looking up at a sky that has suddenly clouded over again. A raindrop hits me in the left eye.

There must have been showers in the past which have consisted of one raindrop and then stopped. Someone at the time must have said, "I think I can feel rain in the air," and everyone else must have thought they were a complete nutter, because the whole shower was over after one drop and nobody else felt a thing. Perhaps this will be just such a shower. I look up hopefully. A raindrop hits me in the right eye.

It pours with rain the entire time I am walking round Ardingly Antiques Fair. Not only don't I buy a book, I don't even see a book. It occurs to me that the ten pounds it cost me to get in is, unquestionably, the worst investment I have made in my life. I find a suitably sized wardrobe and shelter there.

I drive home past 'Sam's Emporium', where the sign outside reads -

OPEN TO MEMBERS OF THE BEXHILL MOUNTAIN
RESCUE TEAM FOR THE OVER EIGHTIES

The shop is empty except for Sam and a little old lady wearing a bobble hat. I carry on to my shop through rain which continues to fall heavily.

The worst thing for bookshops is weather. Any kind of weather. If it's sunny, everyone goes down the beach. If it's raining, everyone stops at home watching television. The only people who prefer to visit bookshops on days like this are BOOKBORES.

Shopkeepers everywhere are a target for bores. They know where you are and the fact that your front door is open. I have always been a particular target for BOOKBORES. In the early days, they actually used to queue up waiting for their turn to bore me.

Only the arrival of my mother-in-law brought about an improvement in this situation. Where I would sit back and let them get on with their boring, my mother-in-law actually used to enjoy their company and answer back. In the end, the bores were finding it difficult to get a word in edgeways. My mother-in-law was far more boring than they could ever hope to be.

Nowadays, BOOKBORES passing my shop make a point of peering through the window to make sure my mother-in-law is nowhere to be seen. If she sees them first, its not unusual for her to chase them down the road in order to tell them about her latest visit to the doctors, or the trouble she's having with her mortgage repayments. BOOKBORES are visibly relieved when they see that it's me who's available for boring on that particular day.

The reason bores prefer rainy weather is that they can expect the undivided attention of the shopkeeper. All I want to do is sit back and see if I can sell any of the books that I bought at auction last week. The face that's peering through the rain covered window obviously has other ideas.

BOOKBORES are bad enough.   B..B..B..BOOKBORES are indescribably worse. I know from experience that the unfortunate gentleman now entering my shop not only has nothing interesting to say, he also needs an incredibly long time to say it.

He walks straight past the books that I bought at auction and starts to b..b..b..bore me. I settle back for an afternoon of listening to the rain going pitter patter pitter patter on my bookshop window, and the voice of a B..B..B..BOOKBORE telling me about the b..b..b..books that he'd like to b..b..b..buy if only he had some m..m..m..money.

R..r..r..roll on f..f..f..five o'clock.

Tuesday 8th October

I have always known the day on which my experiment would finish. That day has now arrived. What has been less certain is the place in which my experiment would finish. I have always felt that my experiment could be judged, not only by the money I am left with after the final transaction, but also by the place in which that final transaction takes place.

I have always hoped that my experiment would end in an auction room. An auction room with class; an auction room with dignity; an auction room where there's the smell of money in the air. Sotheby's is just such an auction room.

Heathfield market is not such an auction room. The only smell in the air at Heathfield market is the smell of stale urine that comes wafting in from the outside toilet. My experiment ends at Heathfield market.

For several weeks now my family has been in a state of extreme excitement. It is almost as if Christmas has come three months early. My wife has even constructed an advent calendar, where all the windows open out onto pictures she has cut from the Argos catalogue.

"Ooh look, it's a microwave oven," announce my children in unison, as my wife opens out this morning's final, last day of the experiment, window.

I leave them at the breakfast table and head for Heathfield.

I have had mixed fortunes in disposing of my Billingshurst and Sevenoaks purchases. They fell into four broad categories -

1) Railway books, which I have sold at a modest profit.
2) Breakers, which Mike Cassidy has assured me he is on his way to look at.
3) A 16th century book, which I have sold for a handsome profit.
4) Dregs, which I can't get anyone to look at, let alone buy.

Out of the £529 I spent at the two auctions, I have so far managed to claw back £503. I have only achieved this because of the 16th century book, which was estimated at £100-£150, but which was knocked down to me for £12.

It has provided me with a substantial profit (I sold it to James), and an optimistic Law 9 of bookselling on which to end the year. This reads -

PERSEVERE LONG ENOUGH IN THE AUCTION ROOMS AND IT IS POSSIBLE TO PICK UP A BARGAIN

How this law operates in a world of high reserves and rings, I don't quite understand. I am grateful to it none the less.

I place the dregs in a box, and deposit them in the Heathfield weekly auction. They have been in my shop for two weeks and nobody has so much as looked at them. I put them in the auction and still nobody looks at them. I watch them throughout pre sale viewing and nobody even goes near them. It comes as a genuine surprise when they sell to Geoff Upton for £24. He could have bought them from my shop for £14.

For two months, I have had £1,948 to dispose of in the secondhand booktrade. I have shown restraint. I have shown cunning. What I am left with after all this restraint and cunning is £1,946. I should have shown more commonsense and left the money in the building society. The final total achieved by my experiment now depends on how much Mike Cassidy is prepared to give me for the breakers.

I am greeted, when I return to my shop, by a message from Mike Cassidy telling me he has changed his mind and won't be coming, and a letter that has been forwarded to me by the Billingshurst auctioneer.

This letter has come originally from the owner of the 16th century book on which I made such a handsome profit. The gist of the letter is that the book was entered in the auction with a reserve of £120. The owner was understandably dismayed when the cheque he received in payment was for £9.47. ('A 16th century book selling for less than the price of a large paperback,' the owner's letter laments.)

The purpose of the letter is contained in its final sentence. It reads - "Please can I have my book back?" For nine months, I have trailed round the auction rooms of southern England. In nine months, I have probably lost more money in the auction rooms than I have made. And finally, after nine months, when I do buy a book I can make a bit of money on, the owner writes to me asking if he can have his book back.

I get out the Tippex and erase all trace of Law 9 from my list of the laws of secondhand bookselling.

I ask James if he still has the book, but apparently he sold it to a dealer with just a hint of an Irish accent. The only suggestion I can make to the book's owner is that he finds out the address of the Black Hole Bookshop and drops them a line there.

It is midnight when I finally prepare to leave my shop. (Even Pain in the Arse gets fed up and goes home at ten thirty.) I linger in the forlorn hope that, even at this late hour, someone with a couple of hundred pounds in their pocket will come searching for breakers in Bohemia Road.

At one minute past midnight, I put up the 'CLOSED' sign on my experiment, and walk home fingering the £1,946 in my pocket (that's my excuse anyway).

Wednesday 9th October

This morning, for the first time in a year, I have no particular reason to get out of bed. I pull the covers over my head and listen to the sounds of a typical English family having breakfast. It could almost be the soundtrack to 'Nightmare on Elm Street'. I feel no desire to join them. I know that when I do venture downstairs, I will have run out of excuses for hanging onto my £1,946. Unless ...... unless ......

Unless, of course, I change my mind and carry on with my experiment for another year. I pick up the latest Bloomsbury catalogue. The estimates seem ridiculously low. There are books here that I would be able to make vast profits on. And if I get a move on, I would just be able to catch ......

Almost before I know what I'm doing, I'm diving into my smelly socks drawer. The socks are there (I don't even need to see them to realise that). A variety of insects staggering around in various stages of asphyxiation are there. My money is not there. In the place where my money should be, there is a note from my wife which reads -

GONE SHOPPING

Downstairs, I find the house is empty. A recording of 'Nightmare on Elm Street' has been left playing on the television. I feel cheated. I have no doubt, whatsoever, that if I could have carried on for another year, I would have made an absolute fortune.

Why, if I could have spent £2,000 and doubled it's value each month, I'd have ended up with a book worth, let me see, £4,000 ... £8,000 ... £16,000 .... 8 million pounds. I don't know where you go to buy a book for 8 million pounds, but it would have been fun looking.

I turn over the television. Russell Grant is telling all us Leos to be careful with money. I switch back to 'Nightmare on Elm Street': the characters are less depressing. All I have to do now is decide what to do with myself for the next year. It isn't easy. Unless ... unless ...

Unless, of course, I start all over again. I search in my pocket for any loose change (that's my excuse anyway). I find 18p. I look down the back of the settee. I find 43p and an out of date copy of the 'Antiques Trade Gazette'. I raid the childrens' piggy banks. I dig frantically in the back garden. I find a total of £2.37. I head for Sam's.

The notice outside Sam's Emporium reads -

DON'T DESPAIR. TRY ELSEWHERE.

I try Michael's. Michael is pricing up the books he bought at Heathfield market. Amongst them is an odd volume of 'Greater London', marked £10. I look pitifully in his direction.

"You can have it for seven."

I somehow manage to look even more pitiful.

"Do you want it for five?"

I shake my head sadly from side to side.

"How much do you want to pay for it then?"

"Two pounds thirty seven."

"Done."

I hand over the money and dance round the shop waving 'Greater London Vol.I' triumphantly over my head. What I know, but Michael doesn't, is that someone in this week's 'Bookdealer' is advertising for just this book.

As soon as I get home, I open my 'Bookdealer', place my finger at the top of the page and begin to read -

Psychoanalysis for normal people

The history of the acute abdomen in rhyme

Poisoning by arseniuretted Hydrogen

Alone with the Hairy Ainu

On bedside urine testing

The politics of breast feeding

Growing unusual fruit

In search of the wallypug

Discovering oil lamps

Golf with a whippy shaft

African creeks I have been up

The obliging elephant

Living with your vicar

Three centuries of corkscrews

Lets be gay

Fascinating walking sticks

Hopefully if I keep looking long enough, I'll get to Greater London eventually. (That's not a book title. Just a mantra I keep repeating to myself.)